CHQ14

Time Traveller

Jenny at Chatsworth

Time Traveller

Jenny at Chatsworth

Stuart Webb

Seven Arches
Publishing

Published in 2013
By Seven Arches Publishing
27, Church Street, Nassington, Peterborough PE8 61QG
www.sevenarchespublishing.co.uk

A catalogue record for this book is available from the British Library.

Design, scans and typesetting by Alan McGlynn.
Cover Illustration by John Bigwood.

Printed in Great Britain.

ISBN 978-0-9567572-5-8

For

Louise and Phoebe

Acknowledgement

A Huge Thank You To William Johnson

William was the winner of our 2010 writing competition. He bought one of the books in our Time Traveller series and picked up a competition entry form at a Waterstones bookshop. William's entry was over 300 words long and suggested a number of incidents that would make a good story line. Stuart Webb, the author, has used some of these suggestions in this book, including the historical person the time traveller meets!

William suggested the grand house at Chatsworth in Derbyshire, the home of the Duke and Duchess of Devonshire as a setting for a book in our time travel adventure series because:

'...lots of people have heard of it. I think it is better if the story is set in a well-known place. It is a very interesting place to visit and you can explore the house and all the gardens too. There has been a house there for a long time and the building is very beautiful...'

William Johnson, aged 12.

‹IF THIS IS THE FIRST TIME YOU HAVE READ ONE OF THE BOOKS THAT RECORDS THE ADVENTURES OF CHILDREN FROM THE TWENTY FIRST CENTURY IN A TIMEZONE DIFFERENT TO TODAY, YOU NEED TO KNOW›

> That SHARP stands for The Scientific History and Art Reclamation Programme.

> That STRAP stands for the Scientific Testing and Recording of Aggression Programme.

> That time slip is something that you might suffer if you travel through time and space, in a similar way to how some people get jet lag when they fly long distances on a jet air liner.

> That if you travel through time and space you are a xrosmonaut.

Prologue

Danny Higgins stared at the words on the screen of his computer. He still couldn't believe he'd typed them. He'd written a number of time travelling adventures now, with himself as the main character, but this was an adventure to top all adventures. Reading through, he spotted a couple of omissions and added the definitions for SHARP – the Scientific History and Arts Reclamation Programme – and STRAP – the Scientific Testing and Recording of Aggression Programme. Such similar names, he thought, yet such different organisations.

After one last proof read, he clicked the upload button and waited impatiently for the progress bar to fill. What was that crazy saying his dad was always spouting about a watched kettle never boiling? He paced his immaculate room, checking everything was as it should be, confirming everything was in its place.

A subtle ping announced that the computer had finally completed its task. Hanging his school uniform in his neatly ordered wardrobe en route, he plonked himself back on his chair and checked the hit counter. The number of people visiting his website had been growing steadily. Not so much as to cause concern, but enough to make him proud that other people wanted to read his work. He'd never really cared for writing, if he was honest. That was his sister's territory. Sports were more his thing. Kicking a ball around the park with Mark and Griff beat going to watch a play any day. Or so he'd thought until recently. Since he'd been writing these time traveller pieces, he'd started to see the attraction of 'putting pen to paper.' Lately, he'd even read a few books that hadn't been set as part of his school homework. They'd been mainly non-fiction, borrowed from his parents' private library, which had seemed to impress their true owners.

He checked the hit counter again. Finding that two more people had viewed his site, he began to wonder what those who read his stories had thought of them. For that matter, he wondered what his family would think if they ever read one. And, as always, he wondered what everyone would think if they only knew they were all true.

CHAPTER 1

Dark Corridor

Jenny was alone in the natural history wing of the museum at night when somebody turned out the light.

The darkness seemed to descend like a veil across the glass cases of the exhibits, the eyes of the animals within managing one last sparkle of anticipation before they too were enveloped. This was their time now – a time of silence and shadows.

Jenny sat like a statue in a forest of statues, waiting for her eyes to adjust. Maybe wandering off from her class to sketch the occupants of the glass cases hadn't been such a great idea after all? Ever since she'd been small, though, she'd always found it easier to draw when on her own – something her best friend, Bethany, had come to understand and accept. It meant she could focus on what she was doing without worrying whether the person she was with was getting bored, which inevitably meant she totally lost track of time. The museum must be closing. She should have been back with her class ages ago. She tried to look at her watch, but couldn't see the hands, so she fumbled in her bag for her phone. It wasn't there! She'd definitely had it earlier, because she'd sent a text to her mum to reassure her that they'd arrived safely. Mum and dad would go mad if she'd lost it. Well, actually, no, they never lost their temper with her, or her brother, about anything, so it was unlikely, but there was always a first time. After all, the phone *was* practically brand new. Maybe it had fallen from her bag when she'd taken out her sketchbook and pencils. Feeling the darkness with her fingers, hoping to find it lying on the bench beside her, she soon realised her missing phone was the least of her worries. The fact that she was sitting in an empty museum, unable to see a thing, was a much more pressing concern right now.

Panic rapidly rising in her chest, she forced her eyes to penetrate the blackness before her, and, to her relief, shapes slowly formed amongst the shadows.

When it had been announced in assembly, a sleepover in a museum as part of a school history project had sounded so exciting. She'd been to the museum a number of times before, of course, with her parents and brother, but this promised to be something completely different. When they'd returned to their classroom, there'd been murmurings amongst her friends of midnight feasts and ghost stories; it had all sounded like lots of fun. Now, the fun had well and truly stopped. She was in a ghost story of her own, and from the expressions on the faces of the big cats slowly taking shape around her it was quite possible *she* was on the menu for the midnight feast.

Attempting to remain calm, she kept her breathing even and tried to slow her racing heart. There was nothing to worry about, she told herself. She was in the exact same place she'd been thirty seconds ago, and been perfectly content sketching away. The loss of lighting was the only thing that had changed.

Then one of the long shadows shifted. Instinctively, she turned toward the source, and instantly wished she hadn't. A grotesque hand rested on a glass case, the rest of the person thankfully hidden from view. For a moment, her mind tried to convince her it was just one of the exhibits and a trick of the limited light. But then a finger twitched, the movement somehow repulsive. And that was it. She ran. Giving her hammering heart free reign now, she let it propel her forward as fast as her jelly legs would allow.

She had no idea where she was heading, she just knew she had to get away from the owner of that hideous hand. But as she sprinted at full speed, throat burning, arms aching, she couldn't help her mind drifting back to the reason for her flight. It hadn't been an ugly hand, not in the normal sense of the word. There had just been something odd and unnerving about it. Impossible as it seemed, she realised it had been both large like an adult's and small like a child's at the same time.

Hurtling along the dark corridor of glass cases, the occupants impassively staring on at the spectacle, she thought she saw a door. Turning to the right, she skidded on the polished floor, and then urged her body to set off once more. The surge of adrenalin, which had initially coursed through her veins, was waning now, her muscles beginning to complain and seize. She wasn't the athletic one in the family. That was her brother. Her body just wasn't used to this kind of punishment. Surely she'd put enough distance between her and whatever it was that she'd seen, she reasoned; surely it was safe to slow a little now. Then she heard the sound of someone running behind her, closing fast. She'd never been so scared in all her life. And it was that raw animal fear, above everything else, which spurred her on to one last turn of speed.

She could see the double doors in the distance, a

possible means of escape. Her arms were numb, her legs like lead, but still she forced her body on, concentrating on the goal ahead.

Her pursuer was gaining. She could hear their footfalls mixing with her own. She didn't dare look back, in case the sight sapped what little strength she had left.

The brass handles of the doors were so close she could almost touch them. She reached out a hand in anticipation. The thought they might be locked hadn't even crossed her mind, until her hand grasped the cold metal.

Then she heard a word, a word thrust across the gap between hunter and hunted, a word that caused her to hesitate for a split second, before she pulled at the handles with all her might.

She slipped into the next room, a room just like the one she'd left, only this time animals had been replaced by letters and books. She swivelled, searching for a lock, or something to bar the doors. But there was nothing, not even handles to hold onto.

Through the stained glass panes, she could see the dark outline of a figure approaching fast. The figure was smaller than she'd expected, smaller than her imagination had wanted her to believe. Panting hard, she thought back to the one word her pursuer had spoken: 'Jenny.' And now, as she thought about it, she realised it had been a boy's voice calling her name, not an adult, or … monster. Maybe she was overreacting, maybe it was just one of her friends, maybe she should wait and see who came through the doors?

A hand was placed against the glass of one door, as the other hand no doubt gripped the handle of the other. That, she decided, was definitely not the hand of one of her school friends. Instantly, she was scrambling and stumbling away. She willed her arms to move, her legs to push her forwards. But it was no use. Pausing, even for a moment, had been a mistake. Her burning muscles had stopped responding, they'd had enough, so she turned, taking deep breaths, trying to ready herself for whatever was coming, trying to ready herself for a fight.

The door inched open, and through the gap came a boy – no taller or older than she was. His skin was dark, and in the dim light the colour of his eyes seemed to constantly change, from toffee to chestnut and back again.

'It's OK, Jenny … I'm a friend,' he panted, holding out a phone – her phone – as a token of peace.

Bizarrely, her first thought was not how he'd got

hold of her phone, but how he knew her name. She'd certainly never met the boy before. For one, she would have remembered those weird eyes, if she had. They seemed to hold her, mesmerise her, forcing her muscles to relax, her heart to slow.

'How … how do you know my name?' she stuttered.

'I assure you, we know more about you than just your name, Jenny,' the boy replied. 'We've been watching you for some time.'

Although Jenny knew it should, somehow the statement didn't sound the least bit sinister. She felt so calm now, as if she were on the edge of sleep, the sweetest dream waiting to embrace her.

'You see,' he continued, 'I'm from an organisation called STRAP. We choose children to help us with our work, children with special aptitude, children we know we can trust.'

It was odd; he looked like a boy of her age, but when he spoke, he seemed much older.

'And what exactly is your work?' she found herself asking, although she hadn't intended to speak.

'Time travel,' he stated, as if it were a simple matter of fact.

Jenny's thoughts swam through treacle, slow and

stifled. She knew she should be laughing and walking away from the boy's ludicrous ramblings, but somehow she couldn't.

'Here, take it,' the boy instructed, offering the phone to her once more.

Jenny looked down at the hand extended toward her and instinctively took a step back. It was the hand she'd seen through the glass case, the hand she'd seen through the glass of the door, the hand she'd found so hideous before. Now she looked more closely, she found it wasn't exactly deformed. In fact, everything about it was normal, apart from it having two extra fingers. She checked the other hand, down by his side, and found it was the same. She felt a twinge of guilt then for being so cruel. It was probably just a birth defect, something he'd had to live with all his life.

'Funnily enough,' the boy said, reading her thoughts, '*your* hands look strange to *me* too.'

'What do you mean?' Jenny mumbled, her voice sounding alien to her ears, like somebody else was speaking for her.

'Well, where I come from – what you would call *the future* – most people's hands are like mine. We have them altered at birth. You see, it was proven by Charles Hallworth, around fifty years ago, that six fingers and a thumb is the optimum design, for efficiency.'

She looked up to see if the boy was mocking her, making up tales. And there were those eyes again, those weird yet wonderful eyes, telling her everything was true, everything was going to be all right.

Jenny had always thought she was different, always thought she was cut out for greater things. She had her drawing, yes, but she wanted more. She wanted to experience the worlds she drew from history. She wanted excitement and adventure. In short, she wanted desperately to believe what the boy was telling her, but even with those crazy hands and eyes, she was finding it hard. She just couldn't throw off the underlying feeling that this was some elaborate trick.

'Sorry, this is probably a bit of a shock. After all the running and chasing though, I don't have much time to explain.' He smiled, attempting to soften the words. 'I can see you're still not fully convinced,' he continued. 'That's normal at this stage. If you'll just take your phone, it should help.'

Jenny looked down to see that he still had his arm stretched toward her, with her phone – or one just like it – looking like a toy in the broad palm of his hand. She hesitated. For a moment, she didn't want to take it, in case she touched the hand, but she forced herself to retrieve the phone, and, as she did so, her finger brushed his skin, skin that felt just like hers.

Inspecting the phone closely, she soon realised it wasn't hers after all. It *was* a BlackBerry and appeared to be the same model, but it had three extra buttons. She was just about to hand it back, when the boy spoke again.

'Don't worry, it *is* yours. We've just … modified it a little.'

Determined to prove him wrong, she checked the contacts list and then the photos held in memory. It *was* her phone! But, how could that be possible?

She looked back toward the boy, hoping for answers, or possibly a big 'I got you with my practical joke' smile. Despite all the evidence to the contrary, she hadn't completely given up on hope of a rational explanation.

There was something wrong with her eyes. The world was becoming fuzzy around the edges.

'By the way,' the boy said, his words sounding distant, as if they'd had to travel further than the two metres or so between them, 'please don't tell anyone about our … meeting.' There was a pause, while he seemed to think about something, and then he continued. 'Oh, and with all the excitement, I nearly forgot to tell you my name. It's Anniz. Goodbye.'

Then she realised it wasn't her vision that was the problem, it was the boy who was becoming indistinct and blurry. She watched him fade before her, a glass case, displaying the needlework of Mary, Queen of Scots, becoming visible right through him.

'Just type 10814 into your phone and press the black button,' the now empty air whispered to her. 'And everything will become clear.'

CHAPTER 2

New Secret

Jenny sat in her room, in her home, staring down at the black button on her phone. The black button that hadn't been there before she'd met the boy with the weird eyes and the odd hands. The boy who'd dissolved and drifted away, right in front of her.

In the museum, when Anniz had disappeared, Jenny had just stood staring, for what felt like minutes, at the empty space where he'd been standing. If proof had been needed that his story was true, that he was indeed from the future, that little trick had clinched it. She half wondered whether he'd planned it that way – if the explanation, the extra fingers and the modified phone didn't work, surely fading to nothing couldn't fail to convince her.

After that, she'd found her way back to her class in a daze, not really knowing what was happening around her. She vaguely remembered Bethany asking if she was all right, but she had no idea how she'd replied. It hadn't been until she'd arrived home the next day, in familiar surroundings – the shock of what she'd seen slowly subsiding – that she'd finally started to feel like her old self.

Now was the first time she'd been alone, since the events in the museum, the first time she'd been able to think. Her mum and dad were out at some afternoon lecture on local history at the library and her brother, her 'babysitter,' was locked away in his room, as usual – the only sign he was still alive being the tapping of keys. She could remember when they used to play Monopoly, Cluedo, or a game on his computer together on the rare occasions when their parents went out, and they'd been left with a 'real babysitter.' Now all he wanted to do was write his book, in private – a book that no one had ever seen, a book that Jenny suspected didn't actually exist. He'd become so secretive lately that she wondered whether he'd got hooked on some social networking site or other.

She never kept secrets herself. She didn't see the point. They usually made things worse in the long run anyway, when the person you were trying to keep in the dark finally found out, which inevitably happened, no matter how hard you tried to keep things under wraps. Like the time Bethany 'forgot' to invite her to go shopping with Amelia. If Bethany had told her afterwards, it wouldn't have been so bad. It was the fact that she found out days later through Kirstie Stevens, who'd seen them together, which made her feel betrayed. It had been one of the few times she and Bethany had really argued. They didn't speak to each other for a week as a result.

No, open and honest was her motto. Or, at least, it had been until now. The boy from the future was a new experience. Anniz had instructed her not to tell anyone about their meeting, *making* her keep a secret. Then again, even if she had wanted to tell someone about the events at the museum, who would believe her? Certainly not her mum or dad, as they had very little in the way of imagination. In fact, she often wondered exactly where her artistic side came from.

Still, she felt uncomfortable with the situation the boy had placed her in; she didn't like having her hand forced.

She looked back down at the phone and realised how stupid she'd been. Her mind was obviously still not working one hundred percent. The new buttons were *some* kind of proof she could show someone, to convince them her story was true.

She thought about phoning Bethany, but that was no use, Bethany wouldn't be able to see the buttons. So she opened her door and strode down the landing, intent on telling her brother.

As she knocked on his door, the words Anniz had spoken rang in her ears: 'Please don't tell anyone about our meeting.' Surely that didn't extend to her own family?

'Busy,' was the single word reply.

'But it's—'

'Look, Jen, I'm sorry, but I've just got something important I need to get finished.'

Jenny glared at the closed door, frustration rising, as the tapping of keys beyond the red-painted wood resumed. That's it, she thought. If her brother was so intent on keeping secrets, maybe it *was* time she kept one of her own.

She stomped back to her room, slammed the door, plonked herself on the floor, typed 10814 into her phone and banged the black button, before she had chance to change her mind.

The phone started to vibrate, the screen lifting and growing, as though the phone were projecting it up into the air before her. Stunned, Jenny stared, as text began to appear through swirling blue.

This is Anniz here. You can put the mobile down now. The screen will stay in place until the end of our transmissions, or you can type responses back to me, via the phone, if you wish.

Jenny placed the mobile on her lap, never taking her eyes off the floating screen. The message faded and she watched as the background of swirling colour, more intense than any she'd ever seen before, seemed to spin off the screen into the air around her. The screen cleared for a moment and then more text appeared.

Firstly, I must apologise. I should have introduced myself in a less dramatic fashion. Also, I should have provided you with better and more convincing arguments as to the reality of time travel. And finally, I should not have returned to my own time in front of you, on my first visit, as I'm told it can have short term side effects for you.

It was weird, Jenny thought, as she read the words; somehow, Anniz sounded different. It was almost as though the words weren't from the boy she'd met at all, or as though somebody else were telling him what to say.

You see, like you, I'm a student, but at university not school. So I'm still learning the ropes myself. I was so worried about fitting everything into the short travel window I had that I forgot most of my basic training, and I've been marked down as a result.

Instantly, Jenny felt bad. She'd only ever had one poor school report, and it still upset her to think of it. For a while she'd run with the wrong crowd, trying to be popular instead of working hard, and had paid the penalty. When they'd read her report, it had been the closest her parents had come to shouting at her. Never again had she made that particular mistake. Now, feeling partly responsible for the boy's failure, she picked up her phone and typed:

I'm sorry if I overreacted.

There was a short pause and then a reply appeared.

Don't worry. At least you got in contact. I would have been in big trouble if you'd decided not to join the programme at all. Now, here's the boring bit that everyone has to read before they make their first trip.

Jenny was a little taken aback by this. Had she really agreed to join them just by pressing the black button? Maybe she had. She'd thought that pressing the black button would simply provide more information. Before she had time to think or ask a question though, further text scrolled onto the floating screen.

‹Welcome, Jenny, to STRAP 10814›

What you do with us as a time traveller will be of immense help to the future of the human race. When the collapse of society, as you know it, took place and the Dark Chaos followed, we lost all records of what had happened in the past. Humanity only made it through those terrible times because a few scientifically gifted individuals survived. Now we, that is, the survivors of humanity (who are as one; there are no separate nations anymore), are trying to rediscover history. However, due to the immense amount of power required, we can only go back in time as far as the twenty-first century, and we cannot stay for long. With your help, we can explore a little further.

Wow, Jenny thought, as more words scrolled

onto the screen, this is pretty heavy stuff.

Before your first trip, we will provide you with a small time/space travel bag containing a silver coloured disc. The bag attaches itself to you without any straps or adhesives. Both the bag and the disc are vital for the success of your mission.

The screen changed once more. Now there were flashing numbers, counting down. They slowed and finally came to rest on 2013, before the text scrolled on.

When the opportunity for time travel arrives, your phone will start to vibrate and will do so (intermittently) for two hours; after that the time gate will have closed. Don't worry if it's impossible for you to respond right away; you will get another chance later on. If you are available to travel, key 10814 into your phone and press the black button. We will then tell you as much as we know about your destination and the date of your arrival. Please read the instructions very carefully and memorise what you are told. This will help prevent you seeming out of place in your new time period.

When you are ready to leave, make sure you are not

overlooked by anyone. Clothes inhibit time travel, so wear as little as possible, preferably a swimsuit. Press the time/space travel bag onto your swimsuit. You will find that it sticks quite painlessly. Then press the green button on your phone.

On arrival, take the silver disc from the bag and press it on to your forehead. A thin film will come away and seemingly dissolve into your skin. The film will allow us, here at STRAP, to see and record what you are seeing. Put the silver backing disc into your bag. Also put your mobile into the bag. This is very important. It prevents your mobile from being lost, so you will always be able to return. You will find appropriate clothes for the period waiting for you at the landing site.

Although the people you meet should mistake you for someone they know, it is important that you blend in as much as possible in order to help this process.

Whilst you are there, watch, listen and learn; we need information.

When it is time for you to return, the phone will vibrate. Strip down to your swimsuit, key in 10814 and press the red button. If you are in any danger before then, you can type 10814 and press the red button before the vibrations start. We will be able to transport you back even if you haven't taken off the clothes you are wearing. **This must only be done if you are in great danger.** It uses additional amounts of energy and can be problematic.

Jenny thought back to the museum. Anniz had been fully clothed when he'd travelled back to his own time. Was this the basic training he'd mentioned he'd forgotten, the reason why he'd been marked down? She wanted to ask him, but didn't get chance, as the words were appearing on the screen thick and fast.

When you get back you will find that, although you seem to have been away for hours, in actual fact it has only been a few minutes in your present time. We will contact you, via this phone or your computer, for a debriefing exercise.

It is vitally important that you don't tell anyone, including your friends and family, about STRAP or your time travelling adventures. We are already taking a risk by enlisting your help and letting you join our organisation. The more people who know about us and our work the more chance there is of effecting history itself, which would be disastrous for everyone.

The text faded into the swirling blue, and then more appeared, almost as an afterthought.

In particular, it is most important that you don't tell your brother about your missions. From experience, we've found that sibling rivalry can be a terrible thing. He would no doubt also want to join STRAP, and we don't want to disappoint him. You see, we are very selective with who we approach – we only take the best.

The swirling blue light faded and the screen shrank in size, fitting neatly back onto the front of her mobile. An involuntary shiver coursed her spine. It was almost as though they'd been watching her when she'd knocked on her brother's door earlier.

Then the phone began to vibrate in her hand with a series of pulses she'd never felt before. Surely it couldn't be STRAP getting in touch already with her first travel option, could it?

CHAPTER 3

First Mission

Jenny didn't really have time to think, she just typed 10814 into her phone and pressed the black button, as she'd been instructed to do. The screen grew and changed to the swirling electric blue again, words spinning into focus.

‹Time Zone›
1570.

‹Place›
Derbyshire, England.

‹Landing›
A small wooded area near the village of Edensor.

‹Instructions›
Put on time appropriate clothing.

‹Destination›
Chatsworth House.

‹Conditions›
Warm and sunny.

‹Equipment›
Mobile phone, time/space travel bag containing silver metallic disc.

‹Remember›
›Only wear a swimsuit.
›Press the time/space travel bag onto your swimsuit.
›When you arrive, press the disc with the film on it to your forehead.
›Put the metal backing disc into your bag.
›And most important, put your mobile into the bag! You won't get back without it.

There will be some clothes nearby for you to put on and remember the previous instructions given to you.

Good luck.

The human race is depending on you.

The screen cleared and shrank down to its normal size, leaving Jenny alone in her room. She felt dizzy with fear and excitement. This was all happening too fast. Then, with a mixture of disappointment and relief, she realised she didn't have the time/space travel bag and silver disc. They'd made a mistake. She couldn't go after all, even if she wanted to.

She decided to check around her room, as much as the clutter and mess strewn across the floor would allow, just to be sure. There was nothing new that she could see. She opened her wardrobe door and checked inside. No one else would have spotted anything amiss amongst the chaos of clothes and random relics of her younger years, except Jenny. On one shelf, piled high with toys she hadn't played with for years, but couldn't bring herself to throw away, rested a bag she'd never seen before. She pulled it out and opened it. Inside, something small, round and silver sparkled in the light.

As she changed into her swimsuit, she still wasn't convinced she was going to go through with this. It was as though she were daring herself, seeing how far she would go. She pressed the time/space travel bag to her side, half expecting to feel the butterflies flapping in her stomach through her fingers. When she took her hand away, the bag stayed, weightless, like part of her skin.

And now, she realised, she was ready. There was nothing left to do to delay the decision. Her finger wavered over the green button, adrenalin pumping through her body, making her back ache.

Did she really have the guts to go through with this? Now, standing shaking from cold and dread, she decided she didn't. What had she been thinking? Then, unbidden, STRAP's words drifted back to her: 'The human race is depending on you.' So few words, yet so much meaning. This is madness, she thought, as she watched her trembling finger press the green button.

Immediately, a high pitched whine started. It got louder and louder, as if coming closer and closer, and then... Nothing.

The world dropped away and then rushed up to meet her feet, without her falling a millimetre. And it was a new world beneath her feet, or rather, an old world, a different world.

She was in a dark and silent forest, the tall trees seeming to crowd in around her for a better view of the new arrival. It was only recently her parents had started to allow her to hang out with her friends on her own, and this was exactly the sort of place her dad warned her away from visiting every time she left the house to meet up with Bethany. In fact, this was exactly the sort of place she wouldn't choose to visit whether she was on her own, with friends, or with her parents. Shivering, and not just from the sudden drop in temperature, she scanned around.

She half wondered if something had gone wrong, if only her location had changed. Perhaps she hadn't gone back in time at all. Then, as she was placing her phone in the time/space travel bag, she spotted clothes bundled beneath a bush, clothes from another age.

She was surprised to find a pretty, but tired-looking, dress amongst the odd-looking clothes. The dress had long sleeves that ended in wide open cuffs braided with lace. For some reason, maybe because the time zone STRAP had mentioned was so long ago, she'd assumed she would have to dress in rags.

Slipping on the dress looked easy, working out how to get into the various undergarments first, and in what order, was the tricky part. The surroundings didn't help either. It was too quiet, too sinister. Feeling alone, but as though there were someone out there watching her at the same time, she found her shaking hands fumbling for speed. After a number of attempts, mumbling all the while about how STRAP should give instructions on dressing in the time they sent you to, she eventually used up all the clothes piled in front of her, without cutting off the circulation in one part of her body or another.

After shoving on the black, square-toed shoes, she looked around at the lines of trees, stretching out in every direction. Her heart pounded painfully in her chest, the sound seeming to echo through the forest, announcing her fear. She realised she had no idea which way she should be heading, so she set off toward the area of the woods that looked least dark, hoping this would be the shortest route to the edge of the forest.

The damp air pressed in around her, probing her flesh with its cool fingers, as she stepped through the shadows. Every sound she made was amplified a thousand times in the stillness that surrounded her. She found her pace quickening with each and every stride, her heart racing to keep up. When she did eventually emerge from the woods, the warm sunshine, which washed over her, carried with it a wave of pure relief.

The scene spread out before her was like a drawing from one of her history books at school, only in this drawing the people in the village were moving, the smoke from the chimneys rising, the water in the river flowing. She felt the sudden urge to capture the image, but realised she didn't have her pencils and pad with her.

After letting her eyes take in every last detail of the wide valley below her, she allowed them to drift up across the river to a large house, standing alone in its own grounds. That must be Chatsworth. She'd been there before. Her parents had brought her and her brother years ago. They'd taken them to some sort of farm first, where you could pet the animals, if she remembered rightly. Now she was a little older and a little wiser, she knew that had been to butter them up before dragging them round a historical tour of the house and gardens – the real reason for their visit.

Something didn't look right. It wasn't Chatsworth itself, she decided. Although the house and gardens *were* different, there was something about the size of the building and its setting in the landscape, with the hunting tower up on the hill behind, which looked familiar. No, it was the village she'd first seen when she'd emerged from the woods that looked … out of place. It was a long time ago when she'd visited Chatsworth with her parents and her memory of it was hazy, but she was sure there hadn't been a village you could see from the house, and vice versa.

This was no time for daydreams, she told herself. She had a mission. STRAP had said her destination was Chatsworth House, and she suspected they wanted her to get there as quickly as possible, in order to record as much as she could. And that's when she remembered she hadn't applied the disc from the time/space travel bag.

It took a while, and much struggling, to locate the bag beneath the layers of clothes, never mind extract the disc. Eventually she wrestled it out into the day-light. As STRAP had explained, when she placed it against her forehead, a thin film attached itself to her skin, and then dissolved like a tablet on the tongue, leaving only the backing, which she placed in her dress pocket. She couldn't face trying to manoeuvre it back into the bag just at that moment. She could al-ways see to it when she undressed for the return jour-ney.

After taking a deep breath to steady her nerves, she headed down the hill, and into the village, navi-gating her way toward the bridge across the river.

The sights and smells were so alien to her, as she passed between the houses. It was like she was on an-other planet, not just in another time. And the other thing she found odd were the people who, for the most part, were dressed in little more than the rags she'd expected she would have to wear. They didn't seem to bat an eyelid as she passed, despite her being much more finely dressed than they were. Some nodded and smiled, others simply ignored her. It was as though she'd lived there all her life.

As she approached the bridge, she noticed there was a boy sitting on the rough stone wall, tossing twigs into the water below. When she came closer, he looked her way, a scowl immediately creasing his features.

'About time too!' he said, jumping down from the bridge and setting off toward the house. 'Come on. It wouldn't do to be late on your first day!'

Jenny's mind was racing, processing all the new information. This boy obviously thought he knew her. And from what he'd said, she guessed she was to become a servant at Chatsworth. From the sound of things, however, she was in danger of arriving late, something which happened all too often in her real life. She drove her parents mad whenever she had an appointment with the dentist or doctor. No matter how many times they reminded her, she would always forget, and end up having to get ready in a panicky rush, which inevitably meant she forgot something important, making them later still. What was worse, here and now, was that her unintentional tardiness had potentially made this boy late as well.

'I'm sorry if I delayed you,' she said, with feeling. Then she became conscious of the sound of her own voice, the formal words she'd used. Would the boy see through her disguise, see her for who she really was, an interloper from another time?

The boy stopped and stared at her intently, only adding to her concern.

'You *are* a strange one,' he eventually said. 'Always with your 'ead in the clouds and sayin' the oddest things.'

It was weird; she'd travelled through time and space, but in some ways nothing had changed. The boy's description of her was one that had been voiced of her true self a number of times before.

The boy turned and set off again, quickening his pace. Jenny trotted along beside him, worried that she didn't yet know his name, or her own for that matter. She thought about trying to coax them out of him, but then, concerned about the possibility of saying something out of place, she decided it was probably best to speak as little as possible. Fortunately, it was a silence the boy seemed happy to share.

Before reaching the main house, they came to a

round building, set within the wall that surrounded the home within. The boy entered through the open door and she followed on behind. A man working behind a desk inside the single circular room ignored them at first, before finally raising his head.

Jenny didn't know what to do, what to say. She realised that apart from knowing she was a servant and this was her first day, she knew little else. What was her role in the house? Who was she supposed to report to? Maybe she *should* have quizzed the boy on the walk over. She couldn't even introduce herself, as she didn't know her own name. She could feel the heat of embarrassment rising in her cheeks, as she desperately searched for suitable words.

'This is Elisabeth Greene. She's new,' the boy beside her said, saving her blushes.

The man inspected her, grunted and waved them through to the exit at the rear, as he resumed his work.

'Right, I'm off this way,' the boy said, nodding to the left, as they emerged back into daylight. 'You go through the servants' door over there,' he added, pointing down a path leading to the main building.

'Thank you…' she said, the words hanging, waiting for a name she didn't know to complete the sentence, 'so much.'

The boy simply smiled and walked away, with a slight shake of his head. 'I'll maybe see you later,' he called over his shoulder.

She watched him go, wondering whether she would indeed see him again.

Walking toward the imposing building, she noticed, now she was closer, that it bore little resemblance to the present day version she remembered. For one thing, it seemed to have too many floors. There were also square towers near each corner and either side of the central door, which she didn't recollect being there in her own time. And another difference was the servants' entrance, partially hidden behind a large flowering bush.

Before she reached the rather shabby door, it creaked open and a slim, snooty-looking man, who was clearly one of the other servants, ushered her in with an impatient, 'Come on, come on. Hurry up.' As she passed, he added, without even glancing her way, 'I take it you're the new girl. She's out in the gardens, up on the bower.' He left her then, all alone in the small, gloomy hallway, no doubt returning to his duties.

As she searched for a door to the grounds, she replayed the man's words in her mind: 'She's out in the gardens, up on the bower.' But who was 'she' and what the heck was a 'bower'?

When she finally found a way out at the side of the house, an answer to the second question presented itself first. At the centre of one of the ponds, which were spread out between house and river, was a bizarre looking building. Surrounded by water, it stood like a stone island with steps bridging the gap to the mainland. At the top of the steps stood two men, one either side of a doorway, like guards. But guarding what, Jenny found herself thinking. And then she saw, through the gap between the sentries, a lady in a long dress walk by with regal elegance.

This squat, stone tower then was surely the bower the man had mentioned, and the lady in the long dress was no doubt the person she'd been sent to meet. But still, she had no idea who the lady was. Although, saying that, buried deep within her brain, there was a niggling recollection, a memory stored without her knowing, which suggested she knew *exactly* with whom it was she was about to come face to face.

As she crossed the ground, her pace slowing, anticipation and trepidation swirling in her stomach, she told herself she didn't have time for second thoughts.

STRAP was depending on her. In fact, if STRAP was to be believed, the whole of the human race was depending on her, so she took a deep breath and strode up the steps.

When she reached the men at the top, she found they carried weapons at their sides. This brought a new, uncomfortable feeling to her insides, as she wondered whether they would let her pass.

She hesitated, unsure of what to do. The man to her left looked her up and down, and, after apparently determining she was of no threat, gave a curt nod of his head. Taking this as a signal it was safe to proceed, she stepped through the stone doorway and into a room with no walls, no ceiling, just a square carpet of grass for a floor. And the sole occupant of that room with a view was the lady in the long dress she'd glimpsed moments before.

The tall, slender woman stood with her back to her, her tightly curled red hair like coils of fire, flaming in the sunlight. Once again, Jenny felt a jolt of recognition. Somehow, however impossible it seemed, she knew this person.

Slowly, as though time itself had reduced to a crawl, the lady turned to face Jenny, and before the hazel-brown eyes, beneath heavy lids, came to rest on her, she realised how and why she recognised her. It had been in another time, in another place, at the museum when she'd first met Anniz, when she'd seen that face before. With that realisation another came: the men at the entrance were not there to stop people getting in, but to stop this woman from getting out. The men were not guards at all, but jailors.

The sad eyes, which eventually turned her way, showed slight confusion for a second, before the emotion was effortlessly masked.

'Hello,' the lady said, with an attempted smile, which fell way short, 'My name is Mary.'

As Jenny completed the lady's *full* title in her head, the title she'd seen by the lady's picture in the museum, the title of 'Mary, Queen of Scots,' she noticed that something was wrong with the scene before her. Something was very, very wrong.

CHAPTER 4

Hidden Meaning

'Hello, my name is …' Jenny almost said her own name, her real name, before correcting herself at the last minute, 'Elisabeth.'

It was Mary's turn to hesitate.

'How strange,' she eventually said. 'When I first saw you, you reminded me so much of my greatest friend from childhood, back in France. And now I find you share the same first name.'

Jenny was trying to concentrate on the lady in front of her, but was finding it hard. Every time she looked at Mary, something caught her eye, something at the edge of her vision, hovering. Every time she turned her head for a closer look though, it vanished.

'Is something wrong?' Mary asked, glancing over her shoulder. It was clear from her reaction that she didn't see anything out of place.

'No … sorry,' Jenny stuttered, turning back toward her.

There it was again, floating just out of sight, just out of reach. She tried to inspect it, without taking her eyes off Mary. It was a thin dark line, like a scratch or scar hanging in space. And though it was small, it was made conspicuous by the fact it shouldn't have been there. Maybe it was just a side effect of time travel, she tried to tell herself. She remembered the invisible film then, stuck to her forehead, and wondered whether STRAP could see the black line too. She made a mental note to ask STRAP when she returned to her own time.

Then the scar started slowly pulsing, opening and closing, as though it were breathing. Jenny shivered, her skin instantly cold and clammy.

'Come,' Mary said, 'I wish to return indoors. I suddenly feel a chill is in the air, despite the warm rays of the sun.'

Jenny was glad to follow Mary, at what she judged to be a reverential distance, glad to be leaving that unsettling sight behind.

While they were walking though, whenever Jenny looked forward, toward the lady in the long dress, she found the scar returned, trailing Mary at the edge of Jenny's vision.

As they reached the entrance to the bower, the guards – or jailors – filed in line, one in front, one behind. Jenny turned and concentrated hard on the man to the rear to see if a similar effect occurred in the air around him, but all she saw was the man staring back at her with a stern expression, which quickly shifted to suspicion.

'Are you from the village, Elisabeth?' Mary asked, as they headed for the house.

Jenny hadn't expected Mary to ask her such a simple question. After all, she was servant to a queen. Surely, the lady, who'd now matched her pace to Jenny's own, so they strode side by side, should be barking orders at her, not making polite conversation.

'Yes,' she eventually replied. It was a lie of sorts, but one that Jenny justified with the importance of her mission.

'And were you nervous coming to Chatsworth this morning to meet me?'

'A little,' Jenny said, honestly this time.

'But now I'm sure you see there was no need. Chatsworth is nothing more than a building, differing from your own home only by its size. And I am nothing more than flesh and bone, different from you only by virtue of my parents.'

It was weird; in the short time she'd known Mary, despite the age gap between them, she felt relaxed, at ease, as though they were old friends, rather than master and servant.

'Come, we shall return to my room,' Mary said, when they entered the house, 'where we can at least have a little privacy, and the illusion of normality.'

She didn't even glance at the men who escorted them, as she said these words, though Jenny instinctively knew at whom they were aimed. The men, however, maintained their poker faces, not flinching for a second.

After climbing stairs and turning corners until Jenny felt dizzy, they finally came to a set of double doors. The men manoeuvred themselves into their now familiar sentry positions outside the doors, as Mary and Jenny entered the room.

Jenny was surprised to find tables and chairs, where she'd expected wardrobes and a bed. It seemed Mary had a *suite* of rooms, not just the one. This, she assumed, was the result of being a *queen* in custody. Where *normal* people would be held in a bare stone cell, Mary had the surroundings of a monarch, if not the freedom. And with that thought came another: what would become of this woman before her, held against her will?

It was only then that Jenny fully realised where she was. She was living part of history. For better or worse, the events she was witnessing had already occurred, which meant she should know what happened next, she should know how this particular story ended. She should know what became of Mary. She racked her brains, thinking back to history lessons. When she'd first met Mary, she'd recalled that Mary had been kept prisoner on the orders of Elizabeth I, the then Queen of England, but as hard as she tried now, she couldn't remember anything more.

Mary picked up some embroidery and made for a chair. Jenny hesitated, unsure of what she, as a servant, should do next.

'Come, sit with me,' Mary gently instructed, maybe sensing some of Jenny's unease. 'It is good to have someone new to talk to, at last.'

Jenny made for a chair that was close, but not too close, to the Queen and tried to make herself comfortable.

'I have been held captive in a country I thought my friend for so long,' Mary said, deep sadness reflected in her eyes, 'that I find little lifts my spirits these days.' With a sigh, she placed the embroidery back down on the table by her side. 'I even tire of my beloved needlework. Where once it helped me through, by transporting me away, for a short time at least, from the reality of my predicament, now it holds no interest for me. To be honest, I only continue with it, because my jailor's wife, Bess of Hardwick, who sits with me from time to time, loves it so.'

Jenny couldn't imagine what it must be like to be held against your will, unable to do what you wanted, when you wanted. To be trapped in one place, no matter how beautiful it appeared to be at first sight, would no doubt become very dull very quickly.

Jenny found her own heart aching for the sad and lonely lady in front of her. She wanted to help ease the pain, but was struggling to know how. Then a thought, a memory struck her.

'I don't do any needlework, but I do quite a bit of drawing,' she started, before she had too much time to think what she was saying and who she was saying it to. 'And last year, when I was ill in bed, I found I too was getting bored of sketching the same things from around my room over and over again. So, with the help of my best friend, I invented a sort of code.'

She looked over to a see a slight frown creasing Mary's brow. It was clear she didn't fully understand.

'I'd include things in my drawings, you see,' she tried to explain, 'that to everyone else seemed like innocent pictures, but to my friend had a hidden meaning. For instance…' Jenny tried to think of simple examples, whilst being careful to alter them for the time in which she was currently living, 'if there was a ball in the drawing, it meant I was saying something about my brother, who loves … ball games. If I included a rose, it meant I was talking about my mother, who adores flowers. My father would be…' In full flow, she nearly got carried away and said what she'd actually used – a toy car – which would have made no sense at all to Mary, but stopped herself at the last moment, and struggling for a substitute, added, '… a horse … as my father is a farmer.'

When Jenny looked up she saw a smile forming, not just of understanding, but of something more.

'I see in you,' Mary said, 'the same sense of fun and mischief, which I so loved in the Elisabeth I knew in my younger years. We used to play hide and go seek together in the palace gardens, and Elisabeth would invent stories to accompany the game, where we would each play the part of a member of the household – a secret role, which only we knew.' Her eyes glazed over, as her thoughts drifted back to her youth. 'I would give anything for one more of those carefree days, unburdened by the worries of adulthood, released from the pressures of being a queen.'

Although she masked it well, Jenny could see the fear and pain of captivity seeping through the cracks, spreading across the surface of her face. The mist in Mary's eyes, she realised, was not just from memories now.

Jenny felt useless for not knowing what to do, what to say. Then a thought crossed her mind and she found her lips were moving before her brain had formed a meaningful sentence. 'Well, why don't we then?' she asked, her voice almost a whisper, laden as it was with the emotion she was trying so desperately to hide.

Slowly, Mary turned to her, the frown returning. 'What do you mean?'

Jenny's brain was finally catching up with her rogue lips, as she remembered a few occasions recently when, filled with frustration at something that had happened in her ever more complicated life, she'd played with toys she hadn't touched for years. It had immediately transported her back to simpler times and calmed her mind.

'Why don't we forget where we are and why, just for a short time, and play one last game of hide and go seek, of sorts, free from the weight and worries of the world, a game of hide and go seek the guards will never forget?'

The sentence was so eloquent that Jenny was a little shocked to hear it said in her own voice.

A spark Jenny hadn't seen before ignited Mary's eyes, suggesting she knew exactly what Jenny meant. But still, Mary hesitated, clearly torn between the cage of her adult life and the inner child within, straining to be released. She glanced toward the window behind her, before she spoke again. 'It is almost dusk though, and I am not permitted to leave the house after dark.'

Jenny could tell from the tone of Mary's voice that deep down she was desperately hoping her strange new servant wouldn't let this dissuade her.

'Then what are we waiting for?' Jenny said, whilst standing and heading for the door.

CHAPTER 5

Dangerous Game

Once they were out in the gardens, with the two guards staring on suspiciously in the fading light, Jenny began to panic. There were plenty of places to hide from the men, once they were on their own, but the problem was how to give the guards the slip in the first place. She realised then, she hadn't really thought this through. She'd raised Mary's hopes of, albeit brief, freedom, and now she would have to dash them.

Her spiralling thoughts were interrupted by a noise, the sound of someone approaching. She looked up to see the boy she'd met on the bridge earlier staggering down the path toward them, weighed down by what looked like ancient gardening tools, his face smeared with the evidence of his day's work. As he came nearer, a heavy implement she didn't recognise slipped from his grasp and fell to the floor, close to one of the guard's feet.

'Oi, watch what you're doin', you grubby little urchin,' the man sneered.

The boy seemed to stumble, as he bent to retrieve

the tool, spilling the rest of his cargo around the guard's ankles, causing the man to jump back in the most effeminate way. Then, regaining his composure, he grabbed the boy by the scruff of the neck, intent on giving him a piece of his mind, whilst the other stood smirking at the spectacle.

Jenny was about to rush forward and help the boy, to defend him from these bullies, when the boy flashed her a secret smile and a sly wink, which suggested he hadn't tripped by accident at all.

This, she realised, was their one and only chance. She gently pulled at Mary's arm, and they were away, darting between trees and bushes. Jenny risked a glance behind and saw nothing but empty air, so they skipped on, doubling back now and then to mask their trail. Pausing, they crouched behind a shrub, its flowers closing for the night, ready to sleep till dawn. Listening for sounds of pursuit, she heard nothing but their own deep panting breath. They'd done it. They were free. Well, not truly free, the high wall, which ringed the grounds, prevented that, but they were alone, and that was something in itself. She wondered how long it would take the guards to realise they were gone, how long it would be before they raised the alarm, how long before they were found. Looking across at Mary for the first time since they'd bolted, she realised it didn't matter. The smile on her face and the fire in her eyes said it had all been worthwhile, however long it lasted.

The crashing noise of branches being broken followed by heavy footfalls signalled the guards' desperate attempts to track them down. Maybe she'd been wrong. Maybe they were too scared to return to the house and admit they'd lost their charge. Maybe they would try to find them on their own first, to save face and avoid punishment. If that were the case, they were in luck, because, given the amount of noise the guards were making, it was obvious where they were. Jenny nodded at Mary and they dashed off in the opposite direction.

Their feet were like feathers falling upon the ground, as the sound of their pursuers faded into the night, replaced by silence all around. The moon broke from behind clouds as they floated away, bathing them in the palest light.

Mary was laughing, head back as she danced along, and Jenny was laughing too, although she hadn't realised until now.

They were free from something else, Jenny noticed. It may have been a trick of the limited light, but the rip in space, which followed Mary everywhere, was nowhere to be seen.

An archway loomed ahead. Beyond was the walled garden through which she'd arrived earlier that day – had she *really* only been here a few hours? Drunk with the success of their escape, they danced on, despite the lack of cover. It didn't matter now; they were invincible, invisible, ghosts across the grass.

Joining hands, they twirled around roses, pirouetted past pansies, the dew drenched flowers shining silver in the moonlight. The air was so thick with the smell of honeysuckle, it felt like they were gently lifting from the earth as they spun down paths and walkways.

Giggling from exhaustion and exhilaration, they collapsed beneath a stone-built gazebo, just in time to see the sobering sight of the two guards entering the garden, puffing and panting, their eager eyes darting this way and that. Instinctively, Jenny held her breath, lay still upon the cool ground, and moving only her eyes, she saw that Mary was doing the same.

'We're never gonna find 'em!' one of the men said, his voice filled with a mixture of fear and anger. 'We'll 'ave to tell the Earl, organise a proper search party.' And then they moved on, through the archway on the far side of the garden, heading round toward the house.

'You have saved me, Elisabeth,' Mary said, earnestly, once the men were out of earshot. 'Whatever happens next does not matter. This brief release has made me feel as though I can face anything now.'

There was something in Mary's voice, a determination in her eyes, which suggested she was talking about more than just what would happen when they were found.

It brought a lump to Jenny's throat to hear those words, to see that steely look of determination. It almost made her forget where she was, and what was about to happen if she didn't think of something fast.

An idea came to her in a flash, an idea she suspected was from some old film, though she wasn't sure.

'They haven't caught us yet,' she said, standing. 'And they can't punish us if we've done nothing wrong, can they?' She offered a hand to Mary and watched the confusion spread across her face, as the words sunk in. Anticipating a question, and knowing that speed was of the essence if her plan was to work, she added, 'come on, I'll explain on the way.'

So they retraced their steps, Jenny whispering the

details of her scheme to Mary as they crept along. Twice they had to stop and hide behind bushes, as groups with lamps passed them by. More by luck than judgement, Jenny suspected, they made it to the servants' entrance without being detected and slipped inside. Up the back stairs they went, shuffling into the shadows at the slightest sound.

Finally, they made it out onto the landing of the second floor. It was dark, but for the moon's rays slanting through the windows. Jenny had no idea where they were. It was Mary's turn to take *her* hand and lead the way.

Moving like thieves, they hugged close to the walls, freezing at every creaking floorboard. Before they'd had a plan, they'd been carefree, living for the moment, but now they had a possible means of escaping punishment, Jenny felt the pressure of ensuring they weren't caught before they could put it into effect.

After turning what felt like the hundredth corner, Jenny found she recognised the doors before them. They were at Mary's rooms at last.

Moments after they entered and made themselves comfortable, they heard voices approaching – well, one voice, to be exact: female, raised, shouting something about how there might be a clue to Mary's escape route amongst her letters. Then the doors burst open and a powerful looking, middle-aged woman entered, trailed by a slightly younger man, with the two guards from the garden bringing up the rear. The expressions on the faces of the men when they saw Mary and Jenny were a picture of shock and amazement. Although the lady, who Jenny took to be Bess, showed surprise at first, her features quickly changed to suspicion.

'What is the meaning of this?' Bess asked, with the calm, steady voice of authority, whilst the men behind stood mute, lost for words.

'Good evening, Bess, Earl,' Mary said with regal dignity. 'I apologise if there has been any confusion. My maid and I were walking in the gardens when we turned and realised our guards were not with us. I believe they may have been distracted by Tom, the young gardener, at the time. When I realised what had happened, I looked for them, but could not find them. As night was falling, I decided it was best if we returned here, to my room, straight away. I suppose I should have told someone, but I did not want to get the guards into any kind of trouble.'

Jenny was impressed. When she'd told Mary of her plan, it had sounded a little weak, but Mary had delivered the lines like a seasoned actress.

Bess and the Earl turned to the guards, who looked at each other, opened their mouths to speak, then closed them again and finally bowed their heads in shame. As Jenny had suspected, they'd clearly been so intent on giving Tom a hard time, they really hadn't seen them slip away behind the bushes. What else could they do then, given Mary's explanation? From their point of view, it could quite easily have been the truth.

In the time/space travel bag at her waist, Jenny's phone started to vibrate with a now familiar frequency. STRAP's timing couldn't have been worse. There was no way she could get away, even if she wanted to. And she *didn't* want to. She had to know what happened next, before she returned to her own time.

'Very commendable of you, I'm sure,' Bess said, her eyes narrowing with distrust, as she returned them to Mary. 'In future, however, please do not concern yourself with the … welfare of the staff. That is *my* domain.' She turned then and swept from the room. 'I'll deal with you two later,' she added, as she passed the guards. The Earl produced a curt nod and followed his wife, the doors shutting behind them as the nervous looking guards resumed their usual positions.

'I have to go now,' Jenny said, as soon as they were alone.

'Of course, of course,' Mary replied, a little of the sorrow back in her voice, back in her eyes. 'You must return to your family in the village.'

Jenny noticed the slash in the surface of the world was back, pulsing at the corner of her vision. It seemed to have grown. And it may have been her imagination but, she could have sworn she saw something moving inside. Trying to ignore it, she said, 'I'm sorry if I've made Bess angry.'

'Do not worry, I will be fine,' Mary smiled. 'She will calm down, eventually. She always does.' She took Jenny's hands in hers then, looking deep into her soul. 'I meant what I said earlier. You have saved me tonight. You have made me realise that however much they imprison my body, they cannot cage my mind, my spirit.' That steely determination was back, power and purpose radiating from her, the slit at the edge of sight shrinking back in its presence.

'Goodnight Elisabeth.'

'Goodnight.'

Jenny raced down the stairs with differing emotions fighting for space in her heart. She couldn't believe she wouldn't see Mary again. Mary had been so different to what she'd expected; she'd been kind, yet strong, whilst remaining young at heart. She would miss her so much, and it was that affection for Mary which gave rise to a second emotion: concern. There was just something so inexplicably ominous and evil about the scar in space which hung over Mary.

Then, of course, there was Tom. Twice he'd inadvertently helped her. She regretted that she wouldn't have chance to thank him properly for what he'd done, before she left, although, thinking about it, she doubted he would understand what it was she was thanking him for anyway.

Reaching the bottom of the stairs, she began to wonder how much time she had before the phone stopped vibrating. What if the pulsing stopped and never started again? She grasped the handle of the door out to the garden and tugged. It didn't budge. For a moment, she panicked, thoughts of having to strip down to her swimsuit in the hallway flashing through her mind. That would never do though. STRAP had said she should undress where she couldn't be overlooked.

She desperately tugged at the handle again, before noticing the door had been bolted from the inside.

Precious moments later, she finally had the bolts drawn back. She was away, like lightning, streaking through the night. She raced across the garden and through the round building, calling 'goodnight' over her shoulder as she passed the man behind the desk. She didn't know whether he even saw her. Then on she ran into the dark forest opposite, no time for fear or indecision.

She stripped down to her swimsuit as fast as the layers of clothes would allow, and shoved them under a bush. She'd made it; she was going home. Pulling her still pulsing phone from the time/space travel bag, she keyed in 10814 and went to press the red button, just as the vibrations stopped. Immediately, new emotions flooded in, driven by thoughts of her parents, her brother and her friends. With all that had happened at Chatsworth, she'd had no time to realise how much she missed them, until now. Surely she would see them all again? Surely she wouldn't be stuck here forever?

Jenny had never understood crying. Even when her mum would break down in front of a tear-jerker on TV, it wouldn't touch her. Recently though, she'd found her emotions seemed to be getting the better of her. She'd felt like weeping a number of times over the past few weeks, without knowing why. She'd blamed it on the fact she would be leaving St Mark's for secondary school at the end of term, and her group of friends would be going their separate ways, though she wasn't sure that was the real reason.

Now, cold, alone, surrounded by darkness and creaking trees, with no way to get back home, stinging tears formed at the corners of her eyes and drifted down her cheeks.

CHAPTER 6

Missing Future

The tears came thick and fast, but they were tears of joy. Sunlight streamed through the window of her own room, in her own home, in her own time.

Back in the forest, the phone had started pulsing again almost as soon as it stopped. The pause in vibrations had probably only lasted seconds, though it felt like hours. She'd typed in 10814 as quickly as her trembling fingers had allowed and stabbed the red button over and over again. The next thing she'd known, she'd been staring through bleary eyes at her wardrobe instead of the woods.

It was only then she'd realised how foolish she'd been. In her panicked state, she'd completely forgotten STRAP had told her she could use the red button to return, in an emergency, at any time.

'Are you OK in there?' her mum's voice called through the door, bringing Jenny swiftly back to the here and now.

Her mum and dad must have returned while she'd been on her mission.

'Yeah … fine,' she replied, as calmly as she could. 'Don't come in,' she added, 'I'm just … getting changed.'

She listened for her mum's footsteps descending the stairs, before grabbing her dressing gown and rushing to the bathroom. Her head was spinning, her stomach rising. Everything was moving, swaying around her. She made it just in time. She'd never been so sick. It was the kind of feeling she had when forced to sit in the back of the car on a long journey, only ten times worse. At one point, she thought she heard someone moving about on the landing, but she didn't care if they heard her, she just couldn't stop.

When the nausea finally passed, her brain hurt and her muscles ached. Shuffling back to her room, she crumpled onto her bed and let sleep numb the pain.

It was getting dark when she woke. For a moment, she didn't know where she was.

'Jenny, tea's ready.'

Her dad's voice calling up the stairs anchored her to her own house, her own time. She tried to stand, but still felt woozy, so slumped back onto the bed, taking deep breaths. Eventually, she managed to stop the room from spinning long enough to make it to the door and descend the stairs, holding tight to the banister for fear of falling.

As soon as she sat at the dining table with her mum and dad, she was presented with a steaming plate of vegetable lasagne. It was one of her mum's specialities. Normally, Jenny would have lapped it up, but feeling as she did, it was the last thing she wanted to see; it reminded her too much of her time by the toilet.

With a grunt, her brother plonked himself in the seat opposite and began shovelling great forkfuls of food down his throat. Jenny could feel the bile rising up from her stomach once more. She needed to concentrate on something else, so, whilst pushing pasta round her plate, pretending to eat, she thought about what she'd been through in the hours before her sleep – or had it only been minutes in this time? She was so proud of what she'd achieved: not just the fact she'd been brave enough to travel back in time in the first place, but that in some way she'd been able to make Mary's life in captivity a little more bearable. She wondered then, like she had before, what eventually became of her brave Queen of Scots. She could look it up in books, she supposed. Her mum and dad were sure to have something on the subject. The internet was another possibility. Somehow, though, neither option felt right. They were too impersonal, too … removed.

'Could we go to Chatsworth House?' she found herself asking, before she'd really decided to speak.

Her mum and dad stopped mid munch and stared at her, making her feel uncomfortable. Her brother didn't even pause for breath.

'Funnily enough, there's a talk on at Chatsworth tomorrow,' her mum eventually said, 'which dad and I wanted to attend, but didn't think we'd be able to, because we'd be out all day, and we didn't think you'd want to come.' She glanced over at an open magazine on the sideboard and then frowned at Jenny. 'But I suspect you already knew that, didn't you?'

Jenny attempted a smile. She had no idea what her mum was talking about.

'You really are the most thoughtful girl,' her mum added, patting Jenny on the back of the hand.

'*I* don't have to go, do I?' her brother mumbled, whilst mopping his plate with a piece of bread.

'What?' he asked, defensively, when all eyes turned his way. 'I have to finish some homework.'

Jenny was relieved to get back to her room. She hadn't eaten any of her tea, although she'd claimed she had when her dad asked. Her mum had fussed round her then. Checking her temperature with a hand to the forehead, she'd announced Jenny looked 'peaky' and shipped her off for 'an early night.' For once, it was a diagnosis and remedy Jenny was all too ready to accept.

Jenny didn't enjoy the hour-long journey to Chatsworth one little bit. She had to close her eyes for most of it, to stop the world blurring past her window bringing back the small amount of breakfast she'd managed to eat. The sickness she'd felt yesterday had eased a little with a long night's sleep, but was far from gone completely. When they did eventually arrive, she was confused by what she saw, making her head spin even more.

'The village...' she blurted out as they passed a gateway to a collection of houses, complete with church. But it wasn't the buildings themselves that upset her balance, although they had changed considerably from how they'd been in 1570, it was the fact they were in the wrong place.

'Ah, that's Edensor,' her dad started, never wanting to miss an opportunity to educate one of his children on all things historical. 'Originally it was a lot closer to Chatsworth, but the fourth Duke, I think it was, had it moved, because it spoiled the view from the house. You see the village was, and still is, owned by the Duke.'

So she'd been right after all. As impossible as she'd thought it to be at the time, the group of buildings had been moved.

The road swept round the hill to reveal Chatsworth itself. It looked so different, yet somehow the same. The shape of the house had changed completely. It now sprawled across the landscape, as though it had partly melted and then reset, although the grandeur, the statement of wealth was still there.

The car rumbled over the stone bridge across the river. Even that seemed different, as though that too had been moved. She supposed maybe it had. After all, if a whole village could be knocked down and rebuilt somewhere new, just to improve the view, then shifting a bridge a few hundred metres would be no problem whatsoever.

Even the gardens looked different, from the glimpses she'd seen. Certainly, the surrounding wall, which had run right down to the river in 1570, was long gone, and there was a large car park to the left of the house, full of cars. It was just all … wrong.

Jenny was starting to wonder what she was

doing here. So much had changed that she was unlikely to find the connection to Mary she'd been hoping for. Maybe she would have been better off leafing through some dry and lifeless history books back at home after all.

Then something came into view that had her thinking maybe it hadn't been a wasted journey. The ponds on the flat ground between the house and the river had all dried up, but the building which had stood in one, still remained. The bower, where Jenny had first met Mary, stood resolute at the centre of a small circular dusty moat. It was funny that she hadn't even noticed it, when she'd come with her parents before. As they pulled into the car park, which now looked so alien to her eyes, she spotted another reminder of the past. Up on the hillside, rising above the trees, the tall, slender tower had also survived.

If she were to find out what eventually became of Mary, Jenny knew she would have to sit through the lecture with her mum and dad first. She followed them through an entrance into the gardens, where their tickets were taken, and on towards the building itself. Climbing a short flight of stone steps, they entered an old theatre.

When Jenny looked around the beautiful room,

she felt as though she'd travelled back in time once more. The walls were draped in thick red material, the ceiling covered in paintings, still in their gold frames, and the stage itself looked as though it hadn't changed for a hundred years or more. There was a gallery up above at the back. Jenny wandered over to read a sign by the stairs which said Queen Victoria had once watched a play there.

Although everyone else seemed to find it riveting, Jenny found the presentation itself mostly dull and boring. She pulled out her pad and pencils, making small sketches while the words washed over her. It was something about the house being used by a girls' school from North Wales during the Second World War. It seemed to go on forever, and her dad wasn't helping, scribbling away in his notepad, as he always did at these sorts of things. His pen became *most* animated, when the member of staff giving the presentation said that on the evening of the 28th June 1942 two German bombers dived out of the sky and peppered the house with machine gun fire. Thankfully, at the end of the presentation, when the speaker asked if there were any questions, there was silence from the audience.

'Would you like to look round the gardens?' her

mum asked, as they filed out of the theatre.

It was obviously her mum's way of saying thank you to her for sitting through the presentation, but Jenny had other plans. 'I'd prefer to see the house first,' she replied.

So they made their way round the many rooms of Chatsworth, stopping at every piece of information, while her dad took notes. Jenny didn't recognise anything. Everything was too … new. It was a crazy thing to say, but true. Even though the ornate corridors, halls and rooms had obviously changed little in the last few centuries, they still looked nothing like Jenny's memories. Even the layout of the building seemed to have changed. She was just thinking that the link she'd hoped for had been broken long ago, when they came to a sign for the Queen of Scots Rooms.

But when they entered, there was still nothing she recognised. The windows, the walls, the chintzy decoration, it was all wrong. Only the location, on the second floor, looking out over the courtyard, was vaguely familiar. It was only then Jenny realised the significance of that view. No doubt Mary had been given rooms high up on the inside of the building to make escape, or rescue, all the more difficult. The thought brought a swelling to Jenny's throat.

She scanned around, hoping to find something about Mary herself, something that would speak of a happy ending, something to remove her sense of foreboding. Perched on a table, she saw a picture of Mary, although it looked nothing like the beautiful woman she remembered. Moving closer, she read the summary of Mary's life on the card beside the picture.

Finally, she knew Mary's missing future, from way back in the past, and, with that knowledge, an unguarded tear slipped slowly down her cheek.

CHAPTER 7

Torn Space

Jenny collapsed on to her bed, buried her head in her pillow and sobbed. She'd held the emotions back all the way from Chatsworth, but now they came flooding out, and like a damn burst, they came in a torrent.

She just couldn't believe what she'd read on the card in Mary's room. Wasn't it bad enough they'd kept Mary imprisoned in one castle or stately home after another for almost twenty years? Did they really have to execute her? And what exactly was her crime – being a queen rejected by her own people, seeking refuge from a distant relative in a neighbouring land?

Her phone started to pulse on her bedside table. She quickly keyed in 10814 and pressed the black button. As the screen lifted and grew, she wondered whether STRAP would have some words of comfort.

This is Anniz here. I've just received the report from your first mission, and I'm afraid there are a few issues I've been asked to discuss with you.

So much for the comforting words, Jenny thought, wiping the tears from her eyes.

Firstly, you forgot to apply the film to your forehead as soon as you arrived, resulting in minutes of valuable data not being recorded. The second, and more major, issue however is that you left the silver backing disc in your clothes when you returned. This could easily have been discovered, putting the whole programme in jeopardy. Fortunately, we were able to recover the situation, but not without some difficulty and extra effort on our part.

Jenny could feel the tears welling once more as she read the words on the floating screen. How could she have been so careless?

Also, your instructions were to watch, listen and learn. You cannot become too involved with the lives of the people you meet, or attempt to change the path of history. This is very dangerous territory and could have disastrous effects for us all. You are there purely to observe.

Now they were going too far, Jenny decided. Didn't they know what she'd been through? Frustration and anger replaced sadness, as she found herself furiously typing a response, before Anniz had time to say more.

Well, what do you expect? You should have picked somewhere safer for me to arrive, especially on my first trip, and given me instructions on how to put on the clothes, and provided me with directions to Chatsworth.

She was in full stride now, thoughts slipping rapidly into words on the screen.

And what about that creepy split in the sky you didn't warn me about?

There was no reply for some time. Jenny wondered then whether she'd said too much, gone too far.

A split in the sky, you say. What exactly did this split look like?

It was weird; even though only a few words had

appeared on the screen, immediately Jenny felt as though the mood, the atmosphere had changed. The phrasing was different, more controlled, more … adult. Again, she had the feeling that either she was now communicating with someone other than Anniz, or someone else was telling him what to say. She typed her response more slowly, more carefully, adding a little thought to what she said.

It was like a tear in the space around Mary, as though someone had cut a line with scissors, just at the edge of my sight.

Then she remembered something, something she'd thought of when she was on her mission, but forgotten until now.

Couldn't you see it through the film, on your recording?

Again there was a pause, which made Jenny wonder what they were doing, what they were discussing. Surely it was a simple question, with a simple yes or no answer.

No, there was nothing on the recording. It was most likely just a glitch in the system, an anomaly that only you could see. It happens sometimes and is nothing to worry about. It would be very helpful, however, if you could write a full report on what you saw, after your next mission.

After her next mission? Jenny had kind of assumed there wouldn't be a next mission, with all the negative comments on her first.

So you will be sending me back in time again?

Until she'd typed the words, Jenny hadn't realised how much she wanted another mission, which came as a bit of a shock, given the pain and hurt caused by meeting Mary. She tried to tell herself it was because she wanted to make a difference, to help STRAP and future humankind where she could. But that wasn't the full story, she realised. There was something else she couldn't put her finger on, something she wasn't even ready to admit to herself.

Oh yes, we'll definitely be offering you another mission. The good work you performed, fully integrating with

The about turn took Jenny somewhat by surprise. When they'd started the conversation it had been nothing but criticism of her work, now it was all praise. What had caused the change? Before she had chance to think about it more, though, another message appeared on the swirling blue screen, a message that left her reeling.

CHAPTER 8

Second Visit

It was all happening too quickly for comfort. Jenny felt that she hadn't really recovered, mentally or physically, from the last mission, and already STRAP was talking about the next trip back in time. The conversation, via her phone, had ended with Anniz, or whoever she'd been talking to, saying they had her next mission ready to go, and they would be sending through the details in the next few minutes. It was almost as if they were *trying* to keep her off balance, preventing her from having time to think.

And then there'd been the strange conversation about the scar in space. Something didn't quite add up there. They'd asked questions and requested a report, as though it had been of great interest and significance, but then dismissed it as a mere glitch.

As though trying to interrupt her train of thought once more, her phone started to vibrate with the STRAP pattern. She typed in 10814, pressed the black button and allowed the screen to blossom blue in front of her.

Hi Jenny, Anniz here. Sorry if I was a bit hard on you before.

Now Jenny was *convinced* she'd been talking to someone other than Anniz earlier. She watched the screen with interest, not allowing him the easy way out by offering a reply.

I forgot it was your first mission. You see, I'm in contact with a number of children from your time zone, and sometimes I get a little mixed up. I'm sure it will be reflected in my marks.

This was new and interesting information. So, she wasn't the only time travelling youngster. Avoiding the feeble attempt to make her feel bad, and get her back on side, she asked a question instead.

Have any of the other children seen a tear in space on their missions?

There was yet another pause, before a reply appeared.

No, none of the others have reported anything similar.
I really wouldn't worry about it. As we said, it was probably just a glitch in the software. As a result, all the systems have been reset and rebooted. In fact, your next
mission will be a good opportunity to confirm the issue
has been resolved.

She had to hand it to Anniz, or whoever was
pulling the strings, they were clever, always coming
up with a convincing argument.

Would it be possible for you to check on your brother
and parents, before we send your next mission details through – just to make sure you won't be disturbed?

Jenny popped along the landing. The tapping of
fingers on a keyboard greeted her before she reached
her brother's door, and she could hear her parents
downstairs, pointing out the errors in a TV programme on ancient Rome. Returning to her room, she
reported her findings.

Are you sure your brother is in his room – did you
speak to him?

This time it was Jenny's turn to pause before she replied. She was tempted to say something sarcastic, but restrained herself at the last minute.

No, I didn't speak to him, but I could hear him typing on his computer. So yes, he's definitely in there.

Why the sudden interest in her brother's whereabouts, she wondered. Or maybe that was unfair. Maybe she was getting over suspicious, reading things into every question and comment that weren't really there. Maybe they were simply concerned about the possibility of her being disturbed.

OK, good. Here are the details of your next mission. Please read them carefully.

‹Time Zone›
28th June 1942.

‹Place›
Derbyshire, England.

‹Landing›

A small wooded area near the village of Edensor.

‹Instructions›
Put on time appropriate clothing.

‹Destination›
Chatsworth House.

‹Conditions›
Warm and sunny.

‹Equipment›
Mobile phone, time/space travel bag containing silver metallic disc.

‹Remember›
›Only wear a swimsuit.
›Press the time/space travel bag onto your swimsuit
›When you arrive, press the disc with the film on it to your forehead.
›Put the metal backing disc into your bag.
›And most important, put your mobile into the bag! You won't get back without it.

There will be some clothes nearby for you to put on

and remember the previous instructions given to you.

Good luck.

The human race is depending on you.

Jenny's heart leapt. The instructions were exactly the same as last time. They were sending her back to see Mary, Queen of Scots. Then she checked the time zone, and her heart sank. The 28th June 1942. For some reason the date seemed familiar, though she had no idea why. She rechecked the rest of the information, in case there was something else she'd missed. Everything was identical, including the ominous final sentence. What if it were true? What if the future of the human race really did depend on her journeys into the past? Even if she wanted to, could she ever turn STRAP down, and run that risk?

But then again, she was convinced there were things STRAP *wasn't* telling her. For some reason, she was purposely being kept in the dark. She felt as though they didn't fully trust her, a feeling that was truly mutual.

Retrieving the time/space travel bag from her wardrobe, she quickly changed into her swimsuit, before hitting the green button.

Immediately, a high pitched whine started. It got louder and louder, as if coming closer and closer, and then… Nothing.

The world dropped away and then rushed up to meet her feet, without her falling a millimetre. And it was a new world beneath her feet, she realised. Or rather, an old world, a different world.

Despite her complaint to STRAP, she'd expected to land in the same location as last time, deep in the woods. But she hadn't, she'd landed near the edge of the woods, within sight of the village. So maybe they *were* listening to her after all. Squinting down at Edensor, she noted it was the later version of the village, the one swept out of sight of the Duke, round the corner, behind a hill.

Scanning around, she found clothes bundled beneath a bush. They looked like they could be part of some sort of school uniform. Wondering whether she was supposed to be visiting Chatsworth on a school trip, she quickly slipped on the white blouse, black woollen stockings, navy pinafore dress and black lace-up shoes. Dressed and ready to go, she stepped out of the shadows and into the warm sunshine, heading for the road she knew would take her to the house.

Then she remembered the silver disc. Quickly, she darted back beneath the cover of the trees. Fishing in the time/space travel bag beneath her blouse, she retrieved the disc and applied the film to her forehead. Being careful not to drop it in the process, she placed the backing back in the bag, together with her mobile phone.

All jobs completed, she set off for a second time down the grassy bank. Edensor was eerily quiet as she passed, but saying that, she realised she had no idea what time of day it was. All she'd been given was a date – a date that gnawed at her, a date she knew but didn't know why.

The Chatsworth, which was slowly revealed as she strode round the hill, was one she recognised. In fact, the main building itself looked almost identical to the present day version she'd visited with her parents. Only the park and gardens were different, although she couldn't put her finger on where or how exactly.

As she crossed the bridge and climbed the hill, she looked over at Queen Mary's Bower – as the guide book her mum had bought described it – a monument to a great and proud lady.

When she arrived at the main building, she found the place looked deserted. Following the route she'd taken with her parents to enter the house after leaving the lecture, she turned right beneath a great stone archway and headed down the driveway beyond. At the end of the driveway, beside the roundabout made of grass, with the tree at its centre, she came across a car, the only sign the building was inhabited at all. The car looked so old, yet new at the same time, like something out of the classic car magazines her dad sometimes bought.

Knowing the open-fronted porch near the vehicle was the main entrance to this part of the building, she made her way up to the double doors within. As she placed her fingers on the handles, she realised that once again she had no idea who she was or how she was supposed to fit in.

For a moment, she stopped and listened to the silence that surrounded her, broken only by the song of a distant bird. If she concentrated, she imagined she could still hear the river bubbling under the bridge. It was all so peaceful, so calming, as though the world were lulling her to sleep.

Then she opened the doors, and a wall of sound nearly knocked her from her feet.

That's when she finally remembered why she knew the date to which she'd been sent back, and with that realisation, a shiver of fear coursed her spine.

CHAPTER 9

Deadly Knowledge

There were girls everywhere – talking, giggling, streaming along the corridor at the top of steps on the far side of the room – all dressed in the same outfit Jenny was wearing. She'd been right; it was a school uniform.

Then a lady stepped from a door on the left of the entrance hall, and silence descended. The woman was neither tall, nor particularly stern-looking, but carried with her an air of authority. The sea of girls parted as she approached.

'Hello, I'm Miss Smith, your new headmistress. Welcome to Penrhos College,' she said with a smile. 'Have your parents left already?'

'Yes … they were … late for an appointment.' Jenny was slowly getting used to this fibbing lark.

'That's fine. Your luggage arrived yesterday, safe and sound. It's been sent down to your dormitory.' She looked around, as if searching for someone.

'Nancie,' she eventually called over the crowd.

Immediately, a small, slim girl came scampering

over.

'This is the new girl, Joan,' Miss Smith told her. 'She'll be in your dormitory.' The headmistress turned back to Jenny, 'It's all right, no need to look so worried, we're all quite friendly at Penrhos. Nancie, here, will look after you.'

If only the headmistress knew what she knew, Jenny thought, then *she'd* look worried too. When she'd opened the doors to Chatsworth and seen the girls in their school uniforms she'd immediately realised that this was the date the lady had mentioned in the lecture, back in her own time. Today was the day the German bombers came, the German bombers that would pepper the building and grounds with deadly machine gun fire. Jenny desperately wanted to tell the headmistress what was going to happen this evening, to tell her to take the girls somewhere safe and not return until morning. But what could she say? She couldn't tell her she'd had some sort of premonition; she would sound hysterical. She tried to remember what they'd said in the lecture. Had anyone been hurt during the attack? Frustrated with herself, she realised she had no idea as she hadn't really been listening.

With another smile, the headmistress turned and left them.

Jenny looked around at the girls milling to and fro, girls who were unaware of the events that were to follow.

'Chatsworth *does* look a little daunting at first,' Nancie said, beside her, misreading Jenny's thoughts. 'Apparently, there are one hundred and seventy five rooms in all. Bucket and Podge tried to count them once, but had to give up at one hundred and twenty three when they were caught out of bounds in the forbidden corridor in Painted Hall. Don't worry, though, you'll soon get used to it. After a month or so, you'll know it like the back of your hand.' Stepping into the flow of girls, she added, 'Come on, we're dorming in South Gallery. It's this way.'

Girls were heading in all directions. Jenny couldn't believe they all knew where they were going. And, as if to support this thought, she could have sworn she saw a couple of the younger ones rushing back the way they'd come, only moments after she'd seen them the first time, with slightly redder cheeks.

As they turned down endless corridors, passed through countless rooms, ascended various stairs, Jenny was amazed how much larger the house seemed, compared to the tour she'd been on in her own time. She guessed this was partly due to the fact that more rooms were open to the current residents than to present day tourists, and partly because of the speed with which they were travelling. She'd thought her guide had been joking when she'd said it would take a month or so to learn her way around, now she was convinced it would take at least two.

'Here we are,' Nancie announced, 'South Gallery. It's not the best and it's not the worst, but it is home, for this term, at least.' Then, maybe anticipating the question waiting on Jenny's lips, she added, 'We change dorms each term, you see. Checking the list on the notice board to see where you'll be sleeping is the first thing everyone does when they return from holidays. The least popular dorms are the largest, like Dining Room, which has twenty five beds. The smaller ones, sleeping eight girls, are the dorms everyone's hoping for.'

Jenny looked around. 'Gallery' was a very grand term for what appeared to be a corridor filled with sixteen beds and chairs, and a number of shared wardrobes. Like the rest of the rooms they'd passed through, most, but not all, of the treasures had been removed for safekeeping, and the lower part of the walls had been boarded for protection.

As Nancie guided her to an empty bed, she introduced her to the occupants of South Gallery, who were for the most part reading, chatting, or playing with each other's hair, as they passed. She tried to remember their names, and the nicknames, which all the girls seemed to have, but struggled. There were just too many faces, and more girls from other dorms were constantly coming and going, all with their own names and nicknames.

'How many girls are there here?' she asked Nancie, who settled herself on the bed next to Jenny's.

'About two hundred and fifty, I think.' Then seeing the other girls filing out of the dormitory, she stood and added, 'Come on, you'll have to unpack later, I'm afraid. It's time for morning chapel.'

Jenny had a job to keep up with Nancie, who was walking at what seemed to be her normal rapid pace. Without stopping for breath, Nancie pointed out along the route all the dorms and classrooms, together with the subjects taught in each. As well as rooms for English, Arithmetic, Sciences, Art, Languages, Physical Education and Elocution, there seemed to be an inordinate number of areas put aside for music. When asked about this, Nancie explained that when Penrhos had been forced to move from its home in Colwyn Bay, because the Ministry of Food had commandeered the buildings to coordinate feeding Britain during wartime, they had brought twenty six pianos to Chatsworth.

'Penrhos prides itself on its musical ability,' she stated, puffing out her chest, whilst smirking over at Jenny.

Jenny smiled back. She found she'd taken an immediate liking to her tour guide. For one thing, her urgency and enthusiasm took her mind off what was about to happen later that day.

'That's West Hall,' Nancie said, nodding toward a room to their left, as they strode down another corridor. 'That's where Foot Class is held twice a week, after lunch.'

'Foot Class?' Jenny quizzed.

'At the beginning of each term, a doctor inspects the feet of all the girls. Those with flat feet have to perform special exercises. Marj says it's the most boring thing in the world, sitting there turning ankles, bending feet and wriggling toes. Fortunately, I've not been called on to attend that particular class, yet.'

Eventually, following the flow of girls, they came to a large open hall. Long wooden seats with high backs filled the centre of the black and white chequered floor. Behind these, great stone stairs rose from the ground with a girl sat each side of every step. As she was shuffled onto one of the seats, she spotted a sort of balcony, or raised walkway, running along the left side of the room. That, she decided, must be the forbidden corridor Nancie had mentioned. Then her eyes were drawn further up, into another world, a painted world of gods and angels, staring down on her. It was like looking up at heaven.

A hush descended on the assembly as a proud-looking girl carrying a bible, followed by the head-mistress, slowly walked down the wood-panelled stairs in front of them and up on to a raised platform.

During the service, Jenny took her lead from Nancie and the rest of the girls, listening, singing and bowing her head in prayer, in what she hoped were all the right places. Surprisingly, she found the singing to be the most enjoyable part, accompanied as they were by the organ by the fireplace and the choir, who turned out to be the girls positioned on the stone stairs behind them. Her family had never been particularly religious, only attending church for christenings, weddings and funerals, as a rule, but singing hymns in such a magical setting felt somehow uplifting.

The rest of the morning, by comparison, was a little boring. Being forced to attend lessons, on what was weekend for her, was not her idea of fun. To make things worse, the classes themselves were not that different to those in her own time. Although, having to use a pencil all the time, in case you had an accident and damaged the priceless classroom – apparently, only the seniors were trusted with ink – was somewhat of a novelty. Even the teachers were restricted to using special dustless chalk for their old-fashioned blackboards.

The highlight by far came after a lunch of paste sandwiches, when they were allowed to roam the gardens on their own, well, in groups of four anyway. Nancie said this rule had been put in place in case one of the girls got injured – one could stay with her while the other two went for help. Out near a metal fountain in the shape of a tree, which the girls from Penrhos called The Copper Tree, Jenny and Nancie, together with Betty and Liz, two other girls from their dorm, played hide and seek in the rock garden, which was an area populated by enormous boulders, ideal for the sport. It was strange, she'd played a game she wouldn't have dreamed of playing with her own friends twice within a week, and, despite her thoughts regularly drifting toward what was going to happen that evening, once again she found it fun.

It was on the way back to the house, however, hot and relaxed after their energetic game, that she noticed something which poured ice on her veins, making her blood run cold.

CHAPTER 10

White Blood

All through afternoon lessons, Jenny kept trying to convince herself that everything was going to be all right, that nobody would be injured when the German planes came, but the split, the gash, the terrible tear in the sky she'd seen, out of the corner of her eye, above Chatsworth, as they'd walked back from break, suggested otherwise. She'd tried to ignore it, tried to tell herself it was just a glitch as STRAP had said, even though the tear had seemed more than that. It had been like an open wound, drawing her eyes back to the hideous things writhing within, things she wanted to forget. And it had been growing by the minute, a great hovering, pulsing, portent of impending evil. *That was it*, the thought she'd been trying to ignore, trying to deny. It had been exactly how it felt, now she thought about it, when she'd seen the tear in space hanging over Mary, but it had been smaller then, less threatening. Mary's execution – the thought still brought a lump to her throat – had been years in the future when she'd met her, and the split had been small and growing slowly. Maybe the larger it got, the nearer the disaster. Following that theory to its logical conclusion, however, given the size and rapid growth of the tear above Chatsworth, meant something awful was going to happen, and it was going to happen soon.

'Are you all right, Joan?' Nancie asked, as they left the final lesson of the day. 'Are you missing home?'

'Something like that,' Jenny replied honestly.

'Don't worry, it's supper time now, and I find that things always seem better when you've had something to eat.'

This was music to Jenny's ears. If the girls were all inside having supper when the bombers opened fire, they would be as safe from harm as could be.

'Then we all meet up in Painted Hall for evening prayers,' Nancie continued. 'But after that we get to kill some time in the gardens.'

In another situation, Nancie's choice of words might almost have been funny, but not here, not now.

When they arrived in Lower Dining Hall – apparently, there were two dining halls, Upper and Lower – Jenny didn't touch her tea. Spam the other girls called it, and tucked in with vigour. It looked like a slab of meat of dubious origins, mixed with white flecks of something of even more dubious origins, to

Jenny, not that the appearance of the meal was her reason for not eating. No, it was the churning in her stomach that made her lose her appetite. She was now convinced that evil was about to engulf her and the rest of the girls of Penrhos, an evil that not all the staff and students would survive.

The meal had finished. Everyone was clearing away, getting ready to leave, and still the planes hadn't arrived, which meant there was only evening prayers between them and being outside when the bombers attacked. If only she could somehow delay them arriving in the Painted Hall, maybe she could prevent the girls from being in the gardens when the planes opened fire.

There was a glass bottle almost full of milk near the edge of the table. As she rose to leave, taking care to make it look like an accident, Jenny hooked her arm round the neck of the bottle and dragged it towards her. The result was immediate and effective. The milk spurted like white blood across the table and down her clothes, quickly pooling on the floor at her feet. Even though she'd known what was about to happen, she was still surprised at just how drenched she got. So much so, in fact, that she found she didn't need to pretend to look shocked, it just came naturally.

A small, round, bespectacled teacher that Jenny hadn't seen before immediately came scuttling over, tutting and mopping with beetle-like efficiency, whilst dispatching Jenny to collect some clean clothes en route to somewhere called Duchess Bathroom, to tidy herself up.

Jenny had been hoping that Nancie would accompany her, so she could take her time, whilst the rest of the girls waited for her return, but it was another teacher who urged her along.

The teacher wouldn't give her a moment's peace in the bathroom, constantly checking on her progress, then her watch, before telling her to hurry up. By the time she was ushered back into the dining hall, she estimated she'd delayed their progress to evening prayer by no more than five minutes. She hoped it was enough.

'Are you all right?' Nancie asked, with an odd look on her face, as they were marched along at speed.

If Jenny hadn't known better, she'd have thought Nancie suspected something. Maybe she'd noticed the spilling of the milk was not quite the accident Jenny had hoped it seemed.

'Fine, thanks,' she eventually replied, at a loss for what else to say.

When they finally arrived at the Painted Hall, the girls from Upper Dining Hall were already there and, by the way they were fidgeting and whispering, appeared to have been there for some time.

Once they'd been ushered onto seats, Jenny found she couldn't concentrate on the service, she was too nervous, and questions were constantly circling her thoughts, making her brain hurt. When would the bombers arrive? Had she delayed events enough to make the school safe? What should she do if the girls were dismissed to the gardens before the attack began?

She wanted to slip outside to check if the tear in the sky was growing or shrinking, but realised there was no time, no opportunity. Instead, she strained her ears, listening for the sound of engines approaching, but could hear nothing but the drone of the service taking place around her. Miss Edman, the Deputy Headmistress, was conducting prayers at the front. Jenny had never wished for anyone to take their time making a speech so much.

'The peace of God, which passeth all understanding—'

At first, the sound which drowned Miss Edman out was like dropped crockery crashing and smashing down endless stairs, but then it grew and grew, until

Jenny was forced to clamp her hands over her ears. The noise was unbearable, as though the whole house were coming tumbling down around them. She screwed her eyes closed in a feeble attempt to shut it out.

Someone tugged at her arm. It was Nancie beckoning her to follow her and the rest of the girls, who were filing from the room. Surprisingly, everyone seemed very calm and orderly, as if they'd practised for this exact event a million times before. With controlled speed, they left the Painted Hall and descended into what Jenny guessed, from the smell and the presence of the wooden barrels, was the old beer cellar.

And here they sat, huddled together, waiting, wondering what would happen next. Some of the younger girls were clearly frightened, but the older girls comforted them, taking the place of absent mothers.

The deafening noise stopped as abruptly as it started. They didn't move though, waiting for the all clear. Eventually, cream crackers and Bovril were passed along the line.

Jenny found herself moved by the scene which surrounded her. These were children, caught in the midst of a war many probably didn't fully understand, yet, despite their own fears, they took time out to help each other through. There was friendship here, a kind of friendship which she realised was often missing in her own time.

A teacher was standing at the end of the cellar, Jenny noticed, making an announcement. Something about the German planes being shot down over Lincolnshire. Immediately, a great cheer rang round the cellar, and Jenny found herself cheering along, though not for the same reason as the rest of the girls. Hers was a cheer of pure relief.

Slowly, they emerged into daylight and inspected the damage, inside and out. From the sound of the attack, Jenny expected a ruin to be waiting for them, but the building looked more or less as it had when they'd hidden themselves away.

Then Nancie pointed out nicks in the bricks of the outside walls, nicks that hadn't been there before. A moment later, a man Nancie whispered was Mr Shimwell, the Duke's Comptroller – whatever that was – came round the corner carrying the girls' bathing costumes, which he'd taken from the clothes line, riddled with bullet holes. A solemn reminder of what might have been.

Out of the corner of her eye, Jenny could see the

tear above Chatsworth had shrunk to almost nothing.

It was late at night, when she was tucked up in bed, with girls snorting and snoring all round her, that Jenny's phone started to buzz. It felt so loud in the near silence that she thought it would wake the others, so she slipped quickly and quietly down South Gallery, being sure to take the clothes she'd arrived in with her. As she passed Nancie, she paused. In such a short time, she felt they'd become real friends. It had been the same with Mary, on her first mission. She was sad to be leaving, but glad to be going home.

In the white nightdress she was wearing, she felt like a ghost, a ghost from the future gliding through the past. It was surprisingly easy to leave the house behind. Nobody shouted her name; nobody came running out to stop her.

Crossing the ground as quickly as she could, she passed Queen Mary's Bower. She'd done so much here in wartime Britain; she just wished she'd been able to help Mary more. Then STRAP's words of warning came back to her in a rush: 'You cannot become too involved with the lives of the people you meet, or attempt to change the path of history. This is very dangerous territory and could have disastrous effects for us all.'

A feeling of dread washed over her as she stripped down to her swimsuit, under cover of the nearest trees, and keyed 10814 into her phone. Knowing what was about to happen at Chatsworth, she'd just panicked and tried to save the staff and students. What if that wasn't what the person who she'd temporarily replaced would have done? What if she *had* changed history? And what if changing the past had altered the future? Would her home and her family even be there when she pressed the red button on which her finger now rested?

With more than a little trepidation, she decided there was only one way to find out...

CHAPTER 11

Changed History

Jenny quickly scanned around. Her room certainly *looked* the same as when she'd left, but there *was* something wrong: it was too quiet. She felt sick, sick to the core, and she wasn't sure it was just the after effects of time travel once more. The house was completely silent, silent as the grave. In a small home filled with four people there was usually someone moving about, playing music or watching television. She wondered then what her parents thought of the silence coming from her own room, when she was on one of her missions. Maybe they simply thought she was drawing, as that was the only time she ever remained still for any period.

Then she turned and noticed something else was not quite right: her door was open. She was sure she'd closed it before she'd left. So maybe someone had been in her room whilst she'd been away. This thought was almost as disturbing as the lack of sound.

After swiftly dressing, she descended the stairs, searching for normality, seeking out the comfort of her parents. Her mum was outside, hanging washing on the line, her dad planting flowers further down the garden. Everything *seemed* normal here.

She knocked on the window, hoping for a reassuring smile or wave. But the sound of her knuckles on the glass sounded muffled and flat. She tried again, only harder. The effect was the same, her parents ignoring her increasingly desperate efforts to attract their attention. Her heart was racing now, panic making her head light, her thoughts fast and wild. Maybe she'd been right; maybe she *had* changed the past, and in so doing written herself out of the present. Was it possible there was no such person as Jenny in the world she'd returned to?

She tried to open the back door, hoping to call out to her mum and dad. Although she could feel the handle in her grip, it wouldn't budge. Even when she lifted herself from the floor, balancing, it didn't move a millimetre, as if she were light as a feather.

Moving quickly back to the window, she banged the glass with all her might, not caring whether it shattered or not. Finally, her mum stopped pegging out one of her dad's shirts on the line and slowly turned toward the house. Jenny waved her arms and shouted in sheer relief, but her mum simply returned to her task, with a slight shake of the head, no hint of recognition.

Collapsing to the kitchen floor with her back against the cupboard, Jenny let the fear and loneliness take her. Something *had* changed. In this version of events it was as though she were quite literally a shadow of her former self. Tears streamed down her face and dripped silently onto the tiles below.

It was only then she realised what in particular was missing from the background noise in the house she'd returned to: there was no tapping of keys coming from her brother's room. Hope lifted her from the cold floor and propelled her up the stairs. Maybe she could contact her brother, maybe *he* would be able to see her, hear her.

The door to her brother's room was closed when she arrived, the 'No Entry' sign firmly in place on the handle. The door to the bathroom was also closed though, she noticed – it was an unwritten rule that the bathroom door should be left open when the bathroom was not in use, due to the lack of a lock. Unsure of which to try first, she did something she'd never dared do before. She bent down and peered through the keyhole of the door to her brother's room. He was sitting at his desk, typing on his computer, although his fingers hitting the keys didn't seem to make a sound. She found it calmed her slightly just to see her brother was there. Until, out of the corner of her eye, she saw what was hovering above his head. A raw gash floated in space, growing, blossoming, threatening to swallow him whole. No, not growing, she realised with a start, but advancing, coming closer. She stumbled backwards, retreating from the sight, banging into the banister behind her, just as the door in front of her dissolved, the gash passing though it. She glimpsed long spider-fingers within the pulsing tear, before she scrambled away toward the safety of her room.

Before, she'd simply been lost and lonely, but now she was consumed by a deep and primitive fear: a fear that her life, her very existence, was in danger. She glanced over her shoulder as she lurched along the landing. A noise she'd never made before, never heard before, escaped her lips, as she realised the nightmare was following her.

Darting through her doorway, she slapped the wood to slam the door behind her. But apart from a dull thud, there was no reaction from the door at all. Given what she'd just witnessed, it would have made little difference anyway. Her eyes flickered round the room, seeking refuge. There was none. She was trapped; there was no escape. What had she been thinking? Why hadn't she made for the stairs? But then, that would only have prolonged the agony. For some reason, she was unable to move objects in the world she currently occupied, which meant she wouldn't have been able to open a window or door to freedom, even if she'd reached it.

All hope lost, she crumpled to the floor in the corner, amongst her old bears. Maybe she'd been wrong, she tried to convince herself. What if the tear wasn't following her at all – was it possible it would simply pass her room by? The answer to her question came quickly; the tear glided silently through the open doorway, bigger and more terrifying than ever. And with it came a heat, a heat that sucked the very air from the room. Jenny curled tight into a ball, panting for breath, wanting to look away from the hideous sight, but not able to. The tear was no longer a line in space. It was a ragged gaping hole, through which twisted hands and claw-like fingers scrambled for purchase, red eyes gleaming in the darkness beyond. Jenny wanted to scream, but she couldn't get any air into her lungs. She was struggling now to stay conscious. Maybe that was for the best. Maybe the oblivion of sleep was her only way out. She was shaking, she realised, shaking from fear and exhaustion. She let her heavy lids close, hoping her thoughts would be taken from her, before the monstrous thing reached her.

No. No, it wasn't her body shaking, it was her phone pulsing. She forced her eyes to open, her brain to think. Her arms were like lead as she searched her pockets for the phone. It wasn't there. And the split in space was half way across the room, bone-like arms and long nails slashing the air before it.

Then it hit her. The phone was in the bag at her waist. Forcing her complaining muscles to react, she pulled the pulsing phone from its hiding place and tried to process the instructions swimming on the screen. The razor claws were almost on her now, she could feel them sweeping past her cheek. This was her last chance. Instinct took over. She watched her fingers ponderously type 10814. And with her last gasping breath, she willed her thumb to hit the red button.

CHAPTER 12

Burning Question

Jenny kept her eyes closed for the longest time. She'd heard the high pitched whine getting louder and louder, and then stopping. She'd sensed the world dropping away and then rushing up to meet her, but she was unsure what it meant. Pressing the red button was supposed to take you back to your own time, wasn't it? And she'd already been in her own time, hadn't she?

She could breathe again, which was something, and the suffocating heat was gone. Slowly, she allowed her eyes to open. She was in her room. There was no sign of the tear in space. Her door was closed. She could hear the tapping of keys drifting down the landing from her brother's room. She was home. For minutes she just lay on the floor letting that thought sink in.

Finally, when she thought her body would allow it, she rose and tested her hand on the door. She'd never been so relieved to see a door swing open in all her life. Rushing along the landing, she barged into her brother's room.

'I may as well throw that in the bin,' her brother complained with a smile, nodding at the No Entry sign left swinging from the handle. Then his smile turned to a frown of concern. 'You OK, sis?'

'Never felt better,' Jenny replied honestly, skipping from the room, without further explanation.

Descending the stairs as fast as her wobbly legs would carry her, she found her parents in the living room, reading.

'Do you fancy some lunch soon, Jenny?' her mum asked, without lifting her head from her book.

It was such a simple question, but one which left Jenny warm inside. 'Yes,' she lied. After her ordeal, eating was the last thing on her mind, but she didn't want to spoil the moment.

'What are you up to this afternoon?' her dad said, his nose deep in a history book.

'I don't know. Could we do something together, as a family?'

Two faces looked her way in unison. 'That would be nice,' her mum said with a smile, closing her book and rising from her chair. 'Right then, I'll get started on that lunch, I think.'

Convinced everything was as it should be this

time, Jenny headed back upstairs. Her phone started to vibrate as soon as she entered her room.

Plonking herself on her floor, with her back against the door, she typed 10814 and pressed the black button. The screen immediately lifted and grew, words appearing on the swirling blue.

Hi Jenny, Anniz here. Are you alone? Is your brother around?

What was with this constantly asking about her brother? Surely they had more important things to discuss than *his* whereabouts. She tried to calm her temper, before she replied, but didn't fully manage it.

My brother's in his room. And yes I have spoken to him.

Before Anniz could ask another question, Jenny typed the question burning in her own mind.

What happened to me when I first returned to my own time?

The reply came slowly, after much apparent

thought.

It seems our system's problem is not fully resolved. This time it caused a slight loss of synchronisation. You see, you didn't return exactly to your own time, but to a time in your recent past.

Slowly, some of what had happened started to make sense to Jenny. She let her thoughts spill onto the screen, in the form of a question:

And because there was no one for me to take the place of, I had no substance, no weight, and my family couldn't see or hear me?

Exactly. Fortunately, we managed to patch the problem and extract you back to your correct present time.

But hold on a minute, Jenny thought. If that were the case, shouldn't there have been a second version of herself, the real Jenny for that time, in the house? A memory came to her then: when she'd been in the bathroom being ill, after returning from her first mission, she'd thought she'd heard someone moving about on the landing. Was *that* it? Was the person she'd heard outside the bathroom been her phantom self? Was the reason her bedroom door had been open and the bathroom door had been closed when she'd returned out of time, been because the real Jenny had been in the bathroom, being sick? Before she could continue with this dizzying train of thought, more words appeared in front of her.

Now, after a promising start, I'm afraid there's been some negative feedback on your second mission.

Jenny couldn't believe it. Was that it? Was that all the explanation she was going to get for the living hell she'd just been through? And where was the apology for that matter? But while her anger grew, text scrolled into view.

We did warn you after your first trip about the possible effects of changing the course of history. You are there to observe only, no matter what you see or hear, no matter how hard that may be.

Jenny knew her thoughts were being diverted, but she couldn't help rising to the bait.

Well, what was I supposed to do, let all those children go out in the gardens and be shot at by the German planes? Besides, it doesn't seem to have had any effect. Everything seems the same.

She paused for a moment as the words she'd written fully sunk in, before continuing with the conclusion forming in her mind.

So maybe the real Joan would have done the same thing I did.

Time travel is not an exact science with rules and formulas for every eventuality. Small changes can be made to minor events in history with little impact. The ripples these changes make soon dissipate, variations in the surface of time covering its own tracks. But the major, more momentous events must never be meddled with. Averting a disaster here could well cause a sizeable wave of change to spread and grow, causing a tsunami further down the timeline.

Once more, Jenny felt as though she were now talking to someone other than Anniz. She read the words on the screen a second and then a third time, but was still unsure what they were trying to say. Were they saying that her actions in the past had caused the future to alter to match? Or did they mean she should have done nothing at wartime Chatsworth, regardless of the outcome?

Whatever the exact meaning of the words, it was clear STRAP weren't happy with her. In fact, it was possible this was the end of the road. They'd probably already decided they wouldn't be sending her on any more missions.

Only now, with the threat of never travelling in time again hanging over her, did she admit to herself what she hadn't been able to before. Yes, she enjoyed journeying through time and space, and meeting people from the past, but there was more to it than that. There was a feeling when you returned that was hard to describe, hard to put into words. It was a longing, a yearning for more. The reason she'd accepted the second mission, despite the disappointment of the first, the reason she would accept another mission now, despite what had happened on her return from her second, was there was something addictive about heading into unknown adventure.

She typed a response, before they had chance to continue.

I saw another tear.

She hesitated, wondering whether this would be enough to save her from being thrown off the programme, before adding more.

In fact, I've seen two. The first was hovering above Chatsworth House, and the second appeared when I returned out of time.

For reasons she couldn't explain, she didn't mention the fact that the tear above Chatsworth had shrunk to almost nothing when disaster had been averted. She also kept her theory about the tear signifying impending danger to herself. Instead, she fed STRAP what she thought they wanted to hear in order to guarantee another mission.

So you're right, you do still have a systems problem. And, as I'm the only time traveller who can see the tears, I'm the only person who can check whether any fixes have worked.

There was another frustrating pause. It was so

difficult to guess what Anniz, or STRAP, was thinking without being able to see them. Words alone, she realised, are only half the story, they don't convey the accompanying emotions you can read in someone's expression or tone of voice.

Once we have performed a full recalibration of our systems, we will be in contact with a new mission. In the meantime, please could you write a full report on what you saw on both missions?

She'd done it, she'd convinced them to keep her on. Although, saying that, there was a part of her that said it had been too easy. It was as though they were willing to accept *any* of her mistakes, however big or small. Yes, they huffed and puffed about this and that, but there was never any *real* threat of dispensing with her services. What she didn't understand was why. Like every conversation with STRAP, she came away feeling that she hadn't been told the full story, that there was something they were keeping from her, something important.

She realised then she hadn't asked the one question she'd intended to, before her train of thought had been diverted, the one question she couldn't hold back, despite the potential consequences. She quickly typed a reply, before they signed off and the chance was lost.

Yes, I'll get started on the reports right away. Before you go, though, I just had one question. When the latest tear appeared, I could see creatures moving about inside. If the tears are simply due to system glitches, what are the creatures?

The length of time it took STRAP to reply immediately had her doubting the explanation when it eventually came through.

It's possible they're a reflection of your own fears. The systems, in their error, could be enhancing your anxieties and overlaying them onto the past world you're seeing.

She hoped STRAP was wrong, that what she'd seen in the rip in space was nothing to do with her own thoughts. No, it must have been generated by the glitch itself, she told herself. It was surely a result of the systems error that STRAP would fix before her next mission, which meant she would never see that hideous sight again. Half wishing she'd never asked the question in the first place, she tried to convince herself that the main thing was she would be offered another chance to travel through time. And with that resolved, she could now concentrate on the one thing she'd failed to do, the one thing she should have done some time ago.

CHAPTER 13

Old Friend

The museum looked different in daylight. For one, the exhibits seemed much less scary when surrounded by tetchy parents and grumbling kids.

It had taken very little persuasion to convince her own parents to bring her, as part of their 'time as a family.' She suspected they'd be here every day, given the opportunity, especially as her mum was now researching a new book on local history. The big surprise had been her brother had agreed to come along too. They'd all gone their separate ways, however, as soon as they'd stepped through the doors.

She retraced the route she'd taken just a few days before. It seemed shorter when not being stalked by shadows. Passing through the double doors to the spot where she'd first come face to face with Anniz, she stopped, holding her breath. For one awful moment she thought the staff of the museum might have changed the display in the cabinet for something else, making it a wasted journey. To her relief, she found they hadn't.

Mary, Queen of Scots, stared back at her from behind the glass. It was a poor picture, she decided, not because it hadn't captured every detail of her face correctly, but because it hadn't captured the radiant beauty or the inner strength.

Now she was here, she wasn't exactly sure why she'd come. It just felt like the right thing to do. Last time she'd dismissed Mary and her needlework as a little boring. With everything that had happened since, she guessed she felt she owed it to Mary to at least take an interest in her work.

There were many pieces of material embroidered with flowers, animals and stylised letters, the colours still vivid after all the intervening years. Her eyes drifted around the display, not really catching on anything, until they came to rest on words written next to a smaller piece of needlework. She read how Mary's inspiration was drawn from emblem books, which contained pictures and words with double meanings, and books on fables and natural history. She also read how Mary would take pleasure in including hidden messages in her work.

Clearly, Mary had taken Jenny's advice and fought off the boredom by placing secret codes in the embroidery she'd produced. At least she'd made a little difference to Mary's life, by making the years of captivity slightly more bearable, she thought.

The information on the sheet ended by saying that a number of Mary's designs, including the one by the side of the sheet, had never been deciphered. Numerous people had guessed at their meaning, but nobody knew for sure.

Her eyes wandered to the piece of needlework in question. It showed a small white gazebo set in beautiful gardens, with a great house in the background. On the steps of the gazebo lay what looked like two piles of rags. And in the foreground, half hidden by hedges, were two statues, mounted on stone plinths.

With a jolt, she realised she recognised this moonlit scene. The house in the distance was Chatsworth. The rags on the floor of the gazebo were her and Mary. And the statues were the two guards. Only when the picture started to blur and melt did she realise there were tears in her eyes.

But why had Mary produced a picture of their exploits, albeit in code? Could it be that Mary had made it for *her*? Was it possible she'd seen a change in her maid after Jenny had left, known she'd not been from her age, and written a message, in the only way available without detection, for her to read in the future – a sort of thank you note through time? It was highly unlikely, Jenny knew, but a comforting possibility all the same.

'Fascinating, isn't it?'

Jenny swivelled to find an old lady peering into her face. She thought she recognised the woman from somewhere, but couldn't think where.

Defying her advanced years, the old lady turned quickly toward the display.

'You know, Mary, Queen of Scots, was kept a prisoner not too far from here, at Chatsworth House, where I went to school for a time.'

It was the movement more than the words, which jogged Jenny's memory, reminding her why the woman looked so familiar.

Jenny's heart stopped, the room seeming to spin around her, only the old lady in front of her remained fixed, remained still. No, that wasn't quite true; only her face remained in focus. And it was a face which, despite the wrinkles, she found she recognised: the face of Nancie.

It was weird; a few hours had passed for Jenny since they'd last met, but it had been seventy years for Nancie. Only the eyes had survived those decades unscathed. Yes, the shine of youth had been dulled with time, but they were still unmistakably those of her old friend.

She desperately wanted to stay, to talk to Nancie, to find out what had happened to Penrhos after she'd left, to discover what kind of life Nancie had led but, instinctively, she knew she shouldn't. Making friends with the same person twice, seven decades apart, when you'd aged less than a day, no matter how different you looked, sounded like a recipe for disaster. Sometimes, she thought, being a time traveller was far from easy. But then, as she smiled and left with a friendly 'Yes, I know,' a thrill ran down her spine as she realised it was a problem she would just have to get used to.

Epilogue

Danny was worried. His sister, Jenny, was behaving strangely. She wasn't eating, looked pale, and was spending more and more time in her room. He used to say she'd taken a happy pill at birth, but recently she seemed subdued and distant. He'd only noticed it recently, although he suspected it had been going on for a while. He was annoyed with himself that he hadn't spotted that something was wrong earlier, but he'd been too caught up in his own world, performing missions for SHARP, and writing up his time travelling adventures. He'd been so obsessed with finding and helping children who'd been enlisted by the rival, rogue outfit, STRAP, who thought nothing of putting young kids in great danger without any protection, he'd forgotten to look out for his own sister. They'd always been so close in the past. He felt as though he'd let her down, just when she needed him most. Even so, he knew he couldn't just barge into her room and ask her outright what was wrong. She would never stand for that. No, he would just have to keep an eye out for his little sister from now on, and see what she was up to. He just hoped she hadn't gotten herself into something serious, something she couldn't handle.

Collect the other exciting books in the Time Traveller Kids series and discover the history of famous sites in the United Kingdom

Danny's interest in history is zero, but when a mysterious boy, claiming to be from a future organisation called SHARP gets in contact with him on his mobile, Danny agrees to travel back to the Tudor period. Making friends in the long-forgotten past gets him seriously hooked on time travel, not to mention history!

Danny has become an experienced time traveller but this doesn't help him when SHARP's communication systems fail. It is the year 671, the Dark Ages and he is left stranded in the depths of winter when wolves roamed the English countryside and Danny cannot understand a word the strange people speak.

Incredibly musically gifted, Atlanta is entranced by the music of the far-into-the- future humankind. Is this what makes her agree to join the growing band of twenty first century kids who go back in time to gather information for the organisation called SHARP?

When Alex McLean is catapulted back to 1314 by a rival outfit to SHARP, his life is in serious danger. This organisation, called STRAP, do not care if he falls to his death when he joins the desperate band of Scots fighters who did the impossible and scaled the terrifying Rock on which Edinburgh Castle stands to this day.

Jo Kelly's parents, both Oxford Academics, are so busy fussing over her super bright brother, who is a chorister in the world famous Magdalen College choir, that they don't realize they are ignoring Jo. How envious they would be, if they knew that Jo is sent back in time to Oxford 1939 and that she actually meets the legendary C.S. Lewis and J.R. Tolkien.

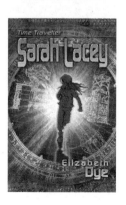

When ten-year-old Sarah accepts the challenge to travel back in time, she thought that she might meet Robin Hood. She had not bargained on joining a band of half-starved children toiling deep under ground in a south Yorkshire coalmine. She becomes a 'trapper' – a child who pulled a string to open a trap to let the trucks of coal hurtle onwards down the tunnel, that is until the mine started flooding. Sarah's life is in danger!

A petrified crowd has gathered at the steps of the magnificent temple of the Emperor Claudius. Their leader tells them that the marauding tribe of Iceni is now less than a day's march from Colchester. All believed that they would be safe inside the temple. Jamie, a boy from the twenty-first century, knows differently.

Atlanta is sent back in time to be with the children working in the danger, dust, and noise of a cotton mill in the North of England. Is time travel addictive? When she visits her aunt in the United States of America, Atlanta agrees to SHARP's offer to travel back to when slaves were brought to America from Africa to toil day after unrelenting day in the cotton fields.

Danny Higgins travels to the amazing, secret world of Bletchley Park to meet the genius, Alan Turing. Danny, clever as he is, has to pass for someone not only totally gifted mathematically but quite a few years older than his actual age. The twist in the story is that SHARP knows all too well how it is that Alan Turing might be the person they need to help them in their fight with their enemy the rogue outfit from the future, STRAP.

The Blog

If you've enjoyed this book, go to Danny's Blog for an exciting FREE read.
www.travellingthroughtimeispossible.wordpress.com/

Competitions And Activities

Seven Arches Publishing often runs competitions for you to enter with prizes of book tokens, that can be spent in any bookshop, for solving puzzles or for a good illustration. Why not go to www.sevenarches-publishing.co.uk and check out whether there is competition or activity on its way based on one or other of our books. We often include the winning entries of our competitions, or the writing, poems or pictures that you send us in the next print run of the title.

Contact Us

You are welcome to contact Seven Arches Publishing
by:
Phone: 0161 4257642
Or
Email: admin@sevenarchespublishing.co.uk